# HABST
## AND THE
## DISNEY SABOTEURS

# LEONARD KINSEY

BAMBOO FOREST

PUBLISHING

ISBN: 978-0-9910079-2-9

Published by Bamboo Forest Publishing
First Printing: April, 2014

Visit us Online at:
www.bambooforestpublishing.com

# ONE

REGINALD "HABST" HABSTERMEISTER pedaled down an empty road towards the Castle. He turned a corner, stopped, squinted into the sun, and choked back a wave of nausea. It was 10AM. He hadn't been up this early in months.

He chained his bike to a light pole near the entrance to the Buena Vista Place apartment complex, pulled his fake ID out of his backpack, slung it around his neck, and walked across the street to the Cast Member parking lot. At the southwest end of the lot was a bus station. Since he'd arrived just after everyone assigned to the final morning shift would have clocked in, the bus stop was empty. He sat at the station, shaded from the sun by a green tarp, and waited. He sweated clear through his shirt.

Habst checked the time on his phone. 10:30AM. Ninety minutes left.

"Stupid busses," he mumbled. "How hard would it be to build some more PeopleMovers?"

The bus finally pulled up. Habst tapped his counterfeit Cast Member ID onto the RFID reader, which turned green. The name on the ID read "Blaine McKinnon". As he boarded, he noticed that the air conditioner was broken. It was hotter in the bus than it was outside.

"Seriously?" he asked the driver.

"At least you don't gotta sit in here all day, buddy," said the old man. "I lost about twenty pounds in the past three hours."

"Sucks to be you," said Habst. He sat down in the first row. Aside from the driver, the bus was empty.

As they departed the station, he checked his phone for the sixth time in as many minutes, trying to memorize his marching orders. The encrypted message he'd received the previous night read:

*Night-vision shot of* Stitch. *Please get two run-thrus – one from each theater. Also, Progress City model. Entrances, electrical, and close-ups of any broken parts. Need it by 12PM EDT. Payment is 2 VTC.*

He locked the phone and put it away as the bus pulled into the station at the Utilidors entrance behind Pinocchio Village Haus.

"Stay cool," he said, exiting the bus.

"Very funny, asshole," said the driver.

Habst walked down the huge sloped ramp into the tunnels and was again overcome with nausea. Whenever the temperature rose over ninety degrees, which happened a lot in Florida, the Utilidors smelled worse than the local dump. The pipes that ferried the trash from the park to the central waste-disposal area were pneumatic, and they weren't exactly airtight. Today they were dispensing a particularly pungent blend of puke and dirty diapers.

He walked as quickly as he could towards Tomorrowland. A golf cart zoomed past him, nearly knocking him down.

"Learn how to drive, dickface!" he yelled.

"Fuck off!" the driver yelled back.

"Eat a bag of cocks, cock!" yelled Habst. "Jerkwad."

"Well that certainly isn't language befitting of a prince," said a sing-songy voice to his left.

He turned and saw Jasmine, dressed in a blue jewel-encrusted bra and matching parachute pants. She twirled a finger through her pitch-black wig, sucked in her exposed stomach and thrust forward her deeply tanned breasts.

"Huh?"

"You're a new 'friend' of Prince Charming, aren't you?"

"What? Where the hell did you get that from?"

"All of the attractive guys down here are face characters!"

Habst stared at her. He was completely oblivious to the fact that she was coming onto him. He was always oblivious when a girl was coming onto him.

"Ooh, and you have Prince Charming's lovely blue eyes, too."

"Do I know you?"

"I don't think so. Would you like to?"

"Uh, maybe? I mean, you seem nice enough. I'm kind of in a hurry, though."

"Well, I'm going on my break, and I could use some help getting out of this costume. The clasp on the bra is really hard to undo."

"That sucks. They should totally be able to help you with that in Costuming, though."

"Oh, okay," said Jasmine.

"I really gotta go. Good luck with that bra!"

Habst turned and quickly walked away, leaving Jasmine standing in the middle of the tunnel.

"Why are all the hot ones gay?!" she yelled, stomping her foot and storming off towards the Mouseketeria.

"What a weird girl," said Habst.

He turned left, and continued his trek to Tomorrowland. After a few minutes the painted stripe on the wall changed from pink to blue, and he reached a familiar stairway. He bounded up the stairs two at a time, went down a dark hallway, opened a door, and was blinded by the harsh Florida sun. Straight ahead was the Tomorrowland Transit Authority PeopleMover, and to his left was Buzz Lightyear's Space

Ranger Spin.

He stashed his fake ID in the front pocket of his backpack and pulled out a stacked bank of four rechargeable Polaroid infrared LED lights. He checked the charge on them and returned them to the backpack. Next, he pulled out his matte black, rooted, and heavily modded HTC One Android phone, switched to the camera app, and made sure the optical image stabilization was enabled and that he had plenty of free storage space. Everything checked out, so he put the phone away and nonchalantly walked over to *Stitch's Great Escape*.

He hated this attraction. The thought of going on it twice depressed him. But 2 VTC meant a full ounce of pot, and that was easily worth two run-thrus.

Not surprisingly, he was the only one in each theater both times. So, twice he powered up his infrared light bank, held it next to his phone, pressed record, and endured ear-splitting sound effects and Stitch's horrible fart burps. While he couldn't see what was going on during the blackouts, his phone could record in the infrared spectrum and pick up everything with incredible detail. Even though he had no idea what he was pointing the camera at, he did his best to get a variety of angles in order to make his benefactor happy.

At the end of the second pass, he stumbled out of the theater into the Merchant of Venus, turned the corner, and entered Cosmic Ray's Starlight Café. Checking his watch, he saw that he still had thirty minutes remaining.

*Plenty of time*, he thought.

He made a beeline for the Topping Bar, where he grabbed a small paper condiment cup, filled it with sautéed mushrooms, squirted hot processed cheese over it, and dumped the entire mess into his mouth. He repeated this six more times, earning a disapproving glare from the Cast Member attending the Topping Bar. He smiled at her charmingly and then walked over to a table across from Sonny Eclipse.

As the show played, Habst scanned through the *Stitch*

videos, and was astounded by how much was going on that was never seen by Guests. The attraction might suck, but these were actually pretty cool behind-the-scenes videos. His one hundred thousand or so subscribers would be thrilled, and hopefully his benefactor would be, too. He opened his YouTube app and started uploading both takes.

He put his Cast Member ID back on and started recording again.

Across from the bathrooms by the patio entrance were two inconspicuous doors. He opened the one on the left, went through it, and walked up a staircase. A roar of white noise grew louder until he reached the top of the stairs, at which point the sound was almost deafening. Massive industrial cooling units filled the vast room. He walked past them towards a small steel ladder bolted to the wall. The ladder was draped in a black cloth.

Still filming, he pulled the cloth aside and climbed up the ladder to a catwalk. He hoisted himself onto the narrow walkway, which was flanked with a scrim that kept light from entering the dark tunnel below, through which the PeopleMovers traveled. On his right was a safety railing, and past the railing was a gorgeous overhead view of Walt Disney's Progress City model.

The model had been built for Walt's 1966 EPCOT (Experimental Prototype Community of Tomorrow) promo film, and then expanded and displayed on the top floor of the *Carousel of Progress* in Disneyland. As originally presented, the model was a futuristic cityscape featuring a massive skyscraper hotel in the center, with PeopleMovers and monorails radiating outward from it. The model was a visual representation of what was to be an urban planning experiment unlike any the world had ever seen.

In fact, EPCOT was the sole reason why Walt had bought so much property in Florida. He had intended to create a new kind of city, where every detail was designed from the ground, and underground, up. In that EPCOT promo film, which was his last filmed appearance, Walt described the city as a project grander and more ambitious than anything he had ever attempted. Tragically, he died soon after announcing the project. Eventually, without his vision and leadership, plans for building the city were abandoned, and EPCOT Center, a theme park, was built instead.

Just as plans for the city itself were scrapped, so was a large part of the Progress City model. At least two-thirds of it had been destroyed when it had been moved from Disneyland to the Magic Kingdom in 1975. And even though the remainder had recently undergone a minor refurbishment, much of it was already in piss-poor condition due to non-existent maintenance. Many of the miniature lights were burned out, and none of the vehicles moved. Paint peeled in places, and there was a layer of dust coating the entire thing that appeared to be an inch thick in places.

The Disney Company had, both figuratively and literally, destroyed a large portion of Walt's unique vision of the future of urban living, and had left the rest to decay through benign neglect.

It made Habst angry. Very angry. He couldn't understand why something so amazingly awesome had been treated so poorly. It was easily the best part of the PeopleMover ride. He'd crane his head at extreme angles as the car whisked past the model, trying to soak in every last detail before it passed out of sight, and desperately hoping the ride would break down in front of it so he could stare at it for longer. He wanted to live in Progress City. It seemed like a place where nothing bad happened, and where technology had solved all of the world's problems....

He filmed the model in great detail, zooming in for close-ups of every building. The camera shook slightly as PeopleMovers passed through the tunnel below.

After ten minutes, Habst walked back across the catwalk,

climbed down the ladder, and went through a door by one of the cooling units. The door opened to a flat wall, which was the model's painted-sky backdrop. A square hole had been cut into the bottom of the backdrop. Habst crawled through the hole and into the underside of the model. He filmed all of the machinery and ancient wires routed under the city, trying his best to trace them back to their junction points. Some of the solder joints at the edge of the model had fallen apart, and wires were dangling free. He saw one arcing against a metal beam.

"Total fire hazard," he said into the camera. "Real nice, Disney."

Satisfied that he'd filmed everything of interest, he stopped recording, opened the YouTube app on his phone, and began uploading the video to his channel, with five minutes left on the clock.

A job well done. Time for a celebratory toke.

Habst walked out of the small room and looked around, verifying that the coast was clear. He was pretty sure nobody ever came up here, as evidenced by a layer of dust on the floor. He confidently pulled a small baggie out of a special airtight compartment in his backpack. The baggie contained a glass pipe, a Colibri lighter, and some OG Kush. He stuffed the pipe, flicked the lighter, inhaled a huge hit, held it for a few seconds, and exhaled into one of the cooling units. The smoke disappeared.

---

DOWNSTAIRS, A SECURITY GUARD passed a vent in the restaurant and sniffed the air. The scent was unmistakable. He pulled out his radio.

"Sam 12, copy?"

"Copy."

"Uh, we've got a fragrant 904 coming from the vents in

Cosmic Ray's. Copy?"

"A *fragrant* 904?"

"10-4. I don't think we have a code for this."

"Ah, okay, copy. Can you trace the source?"

"Well, there are those chillers upstairs…. So…."

"10-4. 514 authorized for chillers. Have a feeling I know exactly who is up there. Dispatching three of the dwarfs to help clean the house. Sam 12 out."

---

UPSTAIRS, HABST PACKED his bowl for the fourth time. The OG Kush was strong, but his tolerance bordered on legendary. He pulled another hit and exhaled just as the security guard walked through the door on the other side of the room.

"Oops," said Habst.

"Hey!" shouted the security guard.

"It's for joint pain, I swear!"

The security guard ran towards him. Habst bolted, scaled the steel ladder on the other side of the room, and ran across the catwalk above the Progress City model. Only then did he remember that it was a dead end.

"Dammit!"

The security guard appeared at the far end of the catwalk, grabbed onto the railing, and bent over, sweat dripping from his face.

"Hey!" he yelled again, gasping for air.

"Can't you say anything else?"

"Get over here, you fucking asshole!"

"C'mon, man! There could be kids down there!"

"Huh?" said the guard. A look of shock came over his face as he felt the rumble of an approaching car and realized the PeopleMover track lay less than ten feet beneath them on the other side of the scrim.

Habst pushed the scrim aside, saw an empty car pulling

into the tunnel, looked back up at the guard, smiled, waved, and jumped off the catwalk into the car below. The guard stood there, flabbergasted, as Habst coasted away through the dark corridor.

"Sam 12?"

"Copy."

"The 904 guy just jumped onto a moving PeopleMover car from the catwalk above that future city model."

"What?! I mean… copy? There's a catwalk up there?"

"10-4. I'm standing on it."

"I'll be damned."

"So… I guess send the dwarfs to the ride exit?"

"10-4. Rerouting dwarfs."

"Good luck."

"Sam 12 out."

Habst saw the guards as soon as the car turned the corner into the long stretch back to the loading platform. There was nowhere for him to go. On this section of the track the drop from the car to the ground was a good twenty feet. He'd never make it.

He pulled off his fake ID, removed his shoe, put the ID in the shoe, and put the shoe back on. It was uncomfortable, but he didn't want to risk a felony charge at this point. He pulled the baggie out of his backpack, ate the gram of OG Kush, threw the pipe over the side of the car into the tree on his left, and pocketed the Colibri. Moments later, the cab pulled into the loading area, where three security guards were waiting for him.

"Well if it isn't Angry, Fatty, and Smelly!" said Habst. "Haven't seen you boys in a while. How're the families? Trailer park still treating you well?"

Fatty and Angry grabbed his arms. Smelly got up in his face.

"Mr. Habstermeister. After all the shit you've given us over the years, you can't imagine how pleased I am to see you right now."

"Jesus. Ever heard of a toothbrush?"

Smelly got even closer and punched him in the stomach. Habst would have doubled over if he wasn't being held tightly by Fatty and Angry. He struggled to catch his breath.

"You jerks are one step below goddamned mall cops."

"Yeah, well these mall cops just nailed your druggie ass," said Angry. "I hope you get locked up and butt raped."

"Dude! What is it with you guys?" Habst said, looking at the small crowd that had formed on the platform. A mother covered her daughter's ears.

Angry looked at the mother and daughter, and turned bright red.

"Get him out of here!"

The guards roughly pulled Habst down the moving walkway. He stood there with them for a second as they descended, and then turned to Fatty.

"You got any snacks? I know you got snacks, dude. Like, maybe some pizza Combos? I love Combos. No joke, man, I'm super hungry. This is cruel and unusual punishment!"

Fatty shook his head as the four of them stepped off the moving walkway. The guards led him past the Tomorrowland Terrace, through a switchback that led backstage, and into the security office on the backside of Main Street.

# Two

"You're banned."

"Nope."

"What? Yes, you're banned."

"No, that doesn't make sense."

"What are you talking about? You got caught!"

"I work here."

"You worked here. Worked. Past tense. You haven't been employed with the Company for nearly a year."

"Yeah, well, I'm still waiting for that CEO position to open up."

"Right. So you don't work here. In fact, if I remember correctly, you were fired for insubordination."

"Which was total bullshit."

"I agree. I took your side on that one. Firing you wasn't my call. But this time, I'm not taking your side. You're no longer a Cast Member, and I told you what would happen if you got caught in an unauthorized area again. And you got caught. Open-and-shut case. You're banned."

"Says who? You don't have the authority to ban me."

"Of course I do, you idiot! I'm the Vice President of Security for the whole resort!"

"So unban me, then."

Charlie Walker literally started pulling his hair out.

"What you don't get, Habst, what you just don't seem to understand, is that if you keep getting caught, and I keep letting you go, then I look like a pushover. I'm the goddamned VP of Security! I need to command a certain level of respect and power!"

"Yeah, okay, I get it, Mister Big-Shot Gestapo Guy. We used to be cool, but now you've sold out. You're an old man controlled by The System. Another one bites the dust. Whatever."

"I'm only seven years older than you!"

'Are you? You seem older. Wow. The Man really got to you, man."

"I'm a detective. I've been in law enforcement my entire adult life. I have medals. It's what I do, and it's what I've always done. There was no 'Man' involved."

"Oh, yeah, the famous detective, saving the world, one urban explorer at a time."

"Don't be a dick. You know what I've been through. What my family went through. You know what this job means to me."

Habst stood up slowly and brushed some imaginary crumbs from his shirt.

"Do I get an appeal?"

"In a year, yeah."

"A whole year?!"

"I told you that last time you got caught. So leave the indignant surprise act at the door. On your way out. As you leave. Which is now. Bye-bye, Habst."

Habst contemplated some act of rebellion, like taking a dump on Charlie's desk. But he'd been backed up for days, and unfortunately a dump would not be forthcoming.

"Do you ever get constipated, Charlie?"

"Yeah. Yeah, I do. Because I have to worry about idiots like you all day."

"There are other idiots like me?"

"No. No, Habst, you're one of a kind."

"Thanks, Charlie. Sorry about all of this."

"Habst, you're twenty-six years old. Why don't you try settling down? Get a job, start a family? Stop smoking pot? You're going to have to grow up sometime. Maybe a year away from this place will be good for you."

"Yeah…. Well…. See ya, Charlie."

"See you in a year. I'm sure you know the way out."

Habst walked out the door and looked onto Main Street from the veranda of the Magic Kingdom's security office. Across the way was the building that used to house the magic store. He'd spent countless hours, and dollars, in that shop as a kid. One time he bought an invisible dog leash there and walked his invisible dog around everywhere for at least six months, much to the dismay of his embarrassed father.

But the magic store was long gone, subsumed into the large gift shop that had eaten its way across Main Street like the Blob.

Further to the right was the façade of the former Penny Arcade. He'd loved the Esmeralda fortune-teller at the entrance of the Arcade. Whenever he'd come to the park as a kid, his first stop was always a visit with Esmeralda to have his fortune told.

But Esmeralda was also long gone, and the Arcade had been gutted to make room for more Vinylmations and t-shirts.

And they wondered why he spent his time exploring backstage. There wasn't anything cool left onstage to discover.

"Screw you and your fancy strip mall, Charlie!" he shouted, running down the steps into the small parking area behind Main Street. He spit on the ground, pulled his fake ID out of his shoe, and walked out past the berm.

# Three

Habst coasted into the circular driveway of a huge mansion just north of the Magic Kingdom. He wearily dropped his bike onto the sparkling pink granite steps, unlocked the gold-trimmed front door, walked into the grand foyer, and flung his backpack halfway down the stairs leading to his room in the basement. The Dell Latitude XFR laptop in the rear compartment cracked loudly against the marble steps. The noise didn't concern Habst in the slightest. The laptop could survive a forty-foot drop onto concrete. He knew this because he'd tested it, repeatedly, and had posted the videos on YouTube to much acclaim and a few hundred dollars in ad revenue.

"Habst, is that you?!" came a screeching voice from upstairs.

He looked at his watch, realized what time it was, and groaned. He sprinted into the kitchen, opened the fridge, grabbed a Heineken, popped the tab, and guzzled the entire can in a few seconds. He rarely drank, and he hated the taste of beer.

"Habst?!"

"Christ," said Habst. He grabbed another Heineken, opened it, brought it to his lips, and then stopped, realizing that too much alcohol would only make it last longer.

"In the kitchen, Ms. Purcelli!"

"Well hello there, handsome," said Ms. Purcelli, slithering into the kitchen. She was wearing a negligee, and reeked of nicotine, booze, and French perfume.

"Hi, Ms. Purcelli. I was just about to take a nap."

"I don't think so, my little boy toy. Monika is at a photo shoot and won't be home for another hour, and I've been thinking of your slim, toned, bronzed figure all day. I'm so wet for you right now, Habst."

"Wow, that's something."

"What will you do with me in that hour, Habst? All sorts of kinky sexy things that dirty young boys like you ache to do? Well, I'm yours. Yours for whatever you desire."

"I already took a huge dump on your chest last week, Ms. Purcelli. I'm not really sure where to go from there."

"You'll think of something."

"Eh, I'm not really in the creative mood, to be honest."

"Well, it won't take you long to pack your belongings, then. And there's also the matter of that huge electrical bill we received last month."

"So you're extorting me for sex again?"

"Exactly."

"You're not a very nice person."

"I don't have to be nice; I'm rich. And you're poor."

"Christ. Okay, fine. How about I have sex with your armpit, and then cum in your nose?"

"Brilliant!" said Ms. Purcelli. "Now carry me up the stairs and ravage me like a beast, you sexy boy!"

"Yes, Ms. Purcelli," he said. He threw her over his shoulder, carried her up the stairs, and paid his bills for another week.

# Four

After a half hour of what could most accurately be described as completely unsexy and awkward unpleasantness involving an unnecessary amount of lube, Habst ran down to his room, leaving Ms. Purcelli to clean up.

Opening the door, he was greeted with the familiar roar of the fans in his 18U rack of virtcoin mining servers. In a single week the servers ate through enough electricity to power a normal household for an entire month, but he didn't give a damn. He wasn't paying for the electricity. Ms. Purcelli was, despite her repeated threats to slap him with the bill.

The white noise from the fans was nearly deafening, and could disguise the sound of even the loudest fart. He sat down, farted loudly, docked his laptop, flipped on his dual monitors, and noted that he'd only mined two virtcoins over the last twenty-four hours. He'd consistently mined three every day for the past two months.

"Dammit!"

He googled "virtcoin difficulty level increase", and sure enough, the difficulty level had increased yet again.

"Total bullshit. No way I'm dumping more cash into this rig," he said, knowing full well that tomorrow he'd order at least two upgraded graphics cards for his servers from Newegg.

Happily, the difficulty increase had caused the exchange

rate to rise. As a result, the coins that had just been delivered to him by his unknown benefactor had substantially increased in value.

Habst opened his Tor browser, typed in the Galt's Gulch address, logged into his account, navigated to his favorite weed seller, and checked out the available strains with the unbridled enthusiasm of a kid in a candy store.

"Hmm, let's see what we have on the menu today…. Blue Dream, Sour Diesel, White Widow, and… oh, sweet Jesus, G-13!"

Habst excitedly read the seller's description of their G-13:

G-13 is a rather infamous strain of weed supposedly developed by the US Government in the 60s. Legend has it that the FBI tried to create marijuana so potent that every pothead in the world would demand it from their dealers. Since the FBI would be the sole grower of this strain, they would inevitably end up selling it to all of the top distributors, at which point a massive bust would be executed, cutting off the head of the drug-trafficking industry. To create this überweed they searched all over the world for the best pot available and crossbred those strains to form a new super-hybrid, the 13th iteration of which was the most powerful. However, their plans were foiled when a rogue lab technician took a cutting from one of the live plants, used it to clone the strain, and made a small fortune selling it to growers across the world.

Their loss is your gain! Toke up and fly away with this super-dank FBI shiznit!

After adding an ounce of the G-13 to his cart, Habst noted the total and transferred the necessary amount of virtcoins from his software wallet to his Galt's Gulch account.

It would take approximately twenty minutes for the transfer to be verified. Habst decided to smoke a bowl while he waited.

He walked to the far end of the basement, lifted his

framed, signed, life-sized poster of Sara Jean Underwood, 2007 Playmate of the Year, off of the wall, and walked into the three-foot by six-foot tunnel behind it. A few feet into the tunnel, he pulled a rock out of the wall, reached into the hole, and pulled out a small safe.

"My baby," said Habst, walking back into the room.

He put his finger on the safe's biometric lock. It clicked, and he opened the box to reveal at least seven ounces of various strains of marijuana, as well as a small glass pipe, rolling papers, a cobalt-colored aluminum grinder, an IOLITE WISPR vaporizer, and a canister of butane. He pulled out a baggie labeled "Northern Lights", dumped a bud into the grinder, ground it up, transferred it into the WISPR's holding chamber, ignited the vaporizer, waited five minutes for it to heat up, and then took a long toke.

He repeated this process until the virtcoins showed up in his Galt's Gulch account, at which point he was pretty blasted. He entered the address of the mansion, with Monika Purcelli as the recipient. He didn't bother to encrypt the address, per the seller's recommended security protocols, and hit the Order button.

Barring interception by law enforcement, which at best would result in a "love letter" from the Postal Service informing him of the seizure of the contents of his package, and at worst would result in a bullshit Controlled Delivery, the ounce of G-13 would arrive in the mail within three days.

He'd never received the infamous seizure notice, but had seen a few other people get them. They varied slightly in content, but followed a similar format. For example:

```
Dear Dreamfinder,

    The purpose of this letter is to advise
you a First Class Package addressed to you
is currently being withheld from delivery
as there are reasonable grounds to believe
```

its contents are non-mailable, and possibly in violation of Federal law, specifically, the Controlled Substances Act. Our attempts to contact the sender to obtain additional information have been unsuccessful thus far. The envelope is approximately 5″ x 7″ and the return address is listed as:

Dreamfinder
200 Epcot Center Dr
Lake Buena Vista, FL 32821

The above described envelope is currently being held at my office. If you want to claim the envelope, please call me at (555) 555-5555 so mutually convenient arrangements can be made for this purpose.

If we do not hear from you or the sender within thirty days of your receipt of this letter, the envelope will be deemed to be abandoned, and it will be disposed of in accordance with U.S. Postal Service policy. If you have any questions concerning this matter, or do not understand the reason this letter is being sent to you, please contact me at the above listed number immediately.

Sincerely,
Postal Inspector

Obviously, only an idiot would actually call the dude and try to reclaim the package. Best course of action was to completely ignore the letter and start getting deliveries to another address.

And Habst had certainly never experienced a Controlled Delivery. A CD, as it was known, was where an undercover Postal Inspector delivered the drugs to your house, waited for you to get them out of your mailbox and bring them inside, and then had the police immediately execute a warrant that let them search your entire house for other drugs and paraphernalia. But even if they did show up with a warrant, Monika was rich, had plausible deniability, and was a minor. He'd bolt through the hidden basement tunnel and exit out of the shed in the back with all traces of his stash in tow, and she'd be let out within the hour with all charges dropped. A truly victimless, albeit inconvenient, crime.

Habst spent a lot of time thinking about this sort of stuff. In fact, virtcoins, weed, and Disney were pretty much all he ever thought about anymore. He'd even considered writing an ebook about how to buy drugs on the Darknet. And, with one exception, Habst had literally spent every virtcoin he'd ever earned on weed, or on a way to get more virtcoins, and thus more weed.

That one exception was a pizza, for which he'd paid a cool 2000 VTC back in 2010. At the time, that amounted to maybe $10. He'd been really hungry and was out of cash, so he posted the following in a Facebook status update: NEED THE COCK. PLZ PM.

He'd only been mildly surprised when he'd received a private message minutes later from an asshole jock who had bullied him in high school. After threatening to publicly shame the jock with screenshots of their conversation, Habst had been able to convince the rabidly homophobic hypocrite to call in an order at the local Domino's. Habst had paid him back in virtcoins, which were essentially worthless to the non-tech-savvy jock.

Today those virtcoins are worth $260,000, and are still sitting unused and forgotten in the jock's virtual wallet. Habst still tells the story of how he spent over a quarter-million dollars on a pizza.

"It was an awesome pizza, man," he always says at the end of the story. "Jalapeños, onions, double bacon, double cheese. Totally worth it."

# FIVE

*THE FOLLOWING ARTICLE is reprinted with permission from The Wall Street Journal:*

August 2, 2012

The Darknet. Onionland. The Deep Web. The Undernet. Child pornographers, drug smugglers, hackers, hit men, Al Qaeda recruiters, weapons traders, and every other sort of seedy black-market raconteurs flock to this backwater pocket of cyberspace, known most commonly by the acronym Tor: The Onion Router. They conduct their business anonymously via customized browsers and private networks, hidden from each other and from law enforcement. Secret websites, all ending in .onion, are passed around to those in the know via encrypted emails. Try typing one of these links in Internet Explorer or Chrome, and nothing comes up. But paste the link into a special Tor browser, and be prepared to experience a World Wide Web filled with a level of depravity and anarchy that would make an experienced 4chan/b/ user blush. If Google, Twitter, and Facebook are the Internet's skyscrapers, townhomes, and ranchers, complete with well-manicured lawns and white picket fences, Tor websites are the city's sewer tunnels, ferrying about all of the feces and rotting trash that normal people don't want to look at or think about.

Originally developed by the US Navy as a tool for covertly passing information to secret agents in countries such as China, where normal Internet traffic is filtered or actively monitored by the Government, Tor was quickly co-opted by cybercriminals. In fact, one of the most popular Tor sites is Galt's Gulch, the Darknet's version of Amazon, where illegal drugs and weapons are listed alongside fake IDs and Kinder eggs, and where sellers receive feedback like on eBay. According to recent estimates, Galt's Gulch brokers over $80 million in annual drug sales. The majority of those transactions are conducted via a relatively new electronic currency: virtcoin.

Virtcoins are essentially chunks of code transferred over the Internet in exchange for goods, services, or actual cash. They are, therefore, a currency just like the dollar or euro, with three key exceptions:

1.  Virtcoins can be "mined" like silver or gold. Any computer that helps process virtcoin transactions is eligible to receive a newly minted virtcoin as a reward. That newly created virtcoin is then said to have been mined. The more transactions you help process, the better your chance of mining a new virtcoin. However, only a certain number of virtcoins are released to be mined per day, and as time goes on the virtcoin protocol changes to make it increasingly more difficult to find them. Each difficulty shift requires a person to use more computers or increase the computational power of their hardware in order to mine the same number of virtcoins as before.

2.  No government controls virtcoins, and thus they are not subject to manipulation by central banks, such as the US Federal Reserve. And, short of shutting down the entire Internet, there is nothing that any government can do to stop virtcoin

transactions. It is a truly free and decentralized currency.

3. Virtcoin transactions are, for all intents and purposes, anonymous. As a result, anything bought or sold with them cannot be traced to the buyer or the seller. All that is visible are the two virtcoin addresses involved in the transaction, which are cryptographic keys made up of thirty-three random characters. These addresses are seen as disposable, and a new one can be used for every transaction a person makes. This anonymity has made virtcoin the currency of choice for purchasing illegal goods or services.

A cryptocurrency like Virtcoin had long been the dream of cypherpunks, activists who promoted the use of cryptography and the Internet as a means of social revolution. But despite the best efforts of countless brilliant programmers and visionary developers, all attempts at creating a viable cryptocurrency had failed.

Until 2008, when an unknown programmer going by the name of Satoru Kobayashi seemingly appeared out of nowhere, setting off one of the most intriguing unsolved mysteries to come out of the digital age....

*Please Turn to Page 13*

# Six

I n November 2010, Habst had posted a video to his YouTube channel showing some backstage areas of the much maligned *The Enchanted Tiki Room – Under New Management*. He'd even climbed into the attic to get a better view of the pneumatics that controlled the movement of the first Iago animatronic, and the pulley-and-gear system that raised and lowered the various props in and out of the Guests' field of view.

While the video did relatively well on YouTube, earning him $80 of Google ad revenue in the first month, he was more pleased by a new arrangement he'd negotiated with a member of HackNCrackBB, a forum he frequented in Onionland.

In December, he'd received a private message in the forum from a user named Sat-Com. It read:

*Liked the* Tiki Room *vid. Got a business proposition. Paid via VTC. If interested, please send public encryption key.*

Having nothing to lose, Habst sent his public key and then promptly forgot about the matter.

A few weeks later he received another message from Sat-Com, this one encrypted. He imported the random mess of characters into Kleopatra, entered his passphrase to decrypt the data with his private key, and read the output:

*Need videos of Utilidors. Complete loop. All entrances to the tunnels from within the park. 2 VTC per 10 minutes of footage. Attached is our encryption key. Please use it for any future communication.*

At the time, one virtcoin was worth about $5. Habst copied the key, imported it into Kleopatra, wrote a message in Notepad, copied it to his clipboard, encrypted it using Sat-Com's public key, and sent it.

*Make it 3 VTC per 10 minutes and you've got a deal.*

A few minutes later, he received a response:

*3 VTC it is. Send us your wallet address. We will be monitoring your YouTube channel.*

"What a weirdo," said Habst. "Why does he keep referring to himself in the royal 'we'?"

But Habst, having nothing better to do, dutifully filmed the entire length of the Utilidors, including the dozens of stairways and doors leading down to the tunnels. The videos lasted a combined total of one hundred and fifty-six minutes. After each one was uploaded to YouTube, Habst received a payout of three virtcoins per ten minutes, for a grand total of 46.8 VTC, which cashed out to approximately $234. In addition, the videos were so well received by the Disney fan community that he made hundreds of dollars in Google ad revenue and gained thousands of subscribers to his channel. Habst was pretty thrilled about this. And, of course, he spent all of the virtcoins on weed, buying an entire ounce of Alien OG once the last payment was made.

---

JUST OVER A MONTH later, the *Tiki Room* caught fire. The official cause was that some old aluminum wiring had overheated and set the thatched roof ablaze. This explanation was universally accepted given the run-down condition of the attraction, and the complete lack of maintenance it had received in the months leading up to the incident.

Luckily, it was a relatively small fire that did minimal structural damage, and the majority of the pneumatic subsystems remained unharmed. However, the first Iago animatronic was completely destroyed. It had been reduced to ashes, almost as if someone had deliberately coated it with napalm and torched it.

This caused an outpouring of virtual high-fives throughout the Disney fan community, most of whom had hated the annoying Gilbert Gottfried-voiced character. Loyal fans much preferred the more sedate original production, which was nearly identical to the version that Walt Disney had commissioned for Disneyland.

Seven months after the fire, the attraction was completely refurbished to address the damaged Iago, and to the fans' delight, it reopened in its original format. While the switch away from the Gilbert Gottfried version was most likely prompted by some offensive jokes the comedian had recently told that got him fired from his Aflac gig, DisNerds latched onto the fire as the instigator. A common joke arose as a result: every time someone complained about the poor state of a Disney attraction, someone else would inevitably say, "Maybe Uncle Walt's ghost will make it catch fire and it'll get a refurb!"

# SEVEN

Habst awoke to Monika giving him a blowjob.

"What the hell, Monika?" he yelled, pulling his limp dick out of her perfectly shaped seventeen-year-old mouth. He jumped out of his chair and accidentally kneed her in her perfectly shaped seventeen-year-old chin.

"Ow!" she yelled.

"Serves you right," he said, pulling up his pants.

"I'm sucking your dick, asshole! Do you know how much any other guy would pay to have me suck their dick?"

Habst perked up.

"No? How much?"

"That was a hypothetical question, douchebag!"

"Well… I mean, you know, it's just that I'm not adverse to the idea, as long as I get a cut."

"Are you seriously offering to pimp me out?!"

"Um…."

"Habst?!"

"Haha, yeah, I'm just joking. Ha."

"It wasn't a funny joke, Habst."

"Right. Not funny. Bad joke."

"And?"

"And… I'm sorry?"

"And?!"

"And… uh… I love you?"

"Thank you. Now pull your pants back down," she said, grabbing the waistband of his jeans.

He smacked her hands away.

"C'mon, Monika, not now. I'm exhausted from being chased by security guards, my stomach hurts from being punched by said security guards, and I haven't taken a shower today so I'm still all sweaty and gross. Can't we wait until tonight?"

She pulled her hands away and pouted, her plump lips turned down and pushed out in a way that was both innocent and extremely hot. It was a look she'd obviously perfected over her years of modeling. Habst had to admit that she was a total sexpot.

"Tonight. I promise."

"Okay, fine," she said. Her pout turned into a smile and she bounced up and down excitedly. "So it sounds like you had an exciting adventure today? Tell me all about it! You know how much your adventures turn me on. So dangerous… so sexy!"

Habst puffed his chest out. He liked that Monika got off on hearing about his exploring. It made him feel like James Bond or Indiana Jones.

He recounted the events of the day to her, embellishing only slightly by having the guard on the catwalk take a few shots at him with his Disney-issued revolver before Habst jumped twenty feet onto the PeopleMover, which was going at least thirty miles per hour at the time.

"Oh, Habst, it's so exciting!" squealed Monika. "You absolutely have to take me on your next adventure!"

"There won't be any more adventures, Monika. Didn't you hear what I just said? I got banned. I'm sure they have my picture plastered up on the homepage of The Hub, and I guarantee you Charlie told all the guards to be on the lookout for me."

"That won't stop my intrepid explorer! You'll find a way to

get back in there, and I'll be right by your side when you do!"

"Yeah… I don't know about that."

"Habst, that wasn't a request, it was a demand. You're going back there, and I'm coming with you. Man up or get the hell out of here!"

Habst sighed. He wished the Purcelli women would stop threatening to kick him out of their house. He needed to find his own place to live. Of course, that would involve finding gainful employment. He wasn't really into that.

"Fine, Monika. I'm sure there will be more Disney adventures, and you can come with me on my next one. Okay?"

Monika let out another high-pitched squeal and bounced around some more. Habst stuck his fingers in his ears.

"Christ. Some day I'm going to record that horrible racket and sell it on Galt's Gulch as a torture device. Now go away. I'm taking a shit and a shower."

Habst stood up and walked into the bathroom, leaving Monika sitting on the floor, pouting again. He closed the door, locked it, pulled down his pants, and sat on the toilet. After ten minutes he gave up. Once again, shits would not be forthcoming. It had been four days since his last bowel movement. He didn't understand where all the shit was hiding. He pressed his stomach, winced, and turned on the shower.

He was in there for a mere thirty seconds before the shower door opened and Monika stepped in, completely nude.

"I picked the lock."

"Well, that was enterprising."

"See, I could be a good sidekick. Picking locks, and distracting security guards with these," she said, pointing at her perky breasts.

"They certainly are distracting."

Against his better judgment, he started getting hard.

"Well look who decided to show up!" said Monika, smiling. "Would your little adventurer like to explore my dark, wet Utilidors?"

She turned around and bent over, showing him her flawless seventeen-year-old ass.

He nodded in resignation. At least there weren't any speeding golf carts in these Utilidors.

# EIGHT

L ATER THAT NIGHT, during a surprisingly crowded run-thru of *Stitch's Great Escape* at the tail end of Extra Magic Hours, something amazing happened in Theater Two.

All was normal until the second blackout towards the end of the show. As usual, the audience was either bored, disgusted, or annoyed. The Cast Members on duty were tired and shell-shocked from having to watch the show on repeat all night. Stitch was back in his teleporter, had fooled the guards, and was about to escape to Florida.

Normally, right after the blackout, Gantu would disable the tracking cannons, which would then twirl around and go limp.

Except this time, everything went completely and totally wrong.

During the thirty-second blackout, somebody had somehow lassoed the two tracking cannons together with heavy-duty rope, cowboy style. This feat was seemingly impossible, since the ends of both cannons weren't easily accessible from any single point in the theater.

Nonetheless, the rope had been given just enough slack that when the cannons made their final twirling motion, a knot formed around the head of the Stitch animatronic and the rope was pulled taut. Then, when the Stitch figure was quickly lowered into the teleportation chamber for his final disappearance, the force of the rapid motion yanked both cannons from their supports, causing them to crash to the ground, and causing the rope to sever Stitch's head.

It was easily the best version of the show that any audience had ever seen.

In the ensuing commotion, the crowd bolted from the theater, screaming and crying, which wasn't a whole lot different from the normal reaction of a crowd leaving that attraction.

---

SECURITY FOOTAGE FROM the preshow displayed nothing out of the ordinary. There were no suspicious characters in the room. Nobody was holding a huge spool of rope. Nobody was dressed like a cowboy.

"Do we really not have infrared security cameras monitoring the theaters?" asked Charlie Walker.

"No sir," answered the Tomorrowland Operations Manager. "The rooms are dark for such a small amount of time that there never seemed to be any need for it."

"Well, it was dark long enough for someone to lasso the goddamned cannons and bring the whole thing crashing down!"

"It doesn't seem possible, sir."

"No…. No, it doesn't," said Charlie. "Something isn't right. This seems like much more than a teenage prank. My gut is telling me that something very strange has happened here…."

# NINE

THE NEXT MORNING, while Monika slept soundly after a night of enjoyable sex, Habst snuck downstairs to check his messages on HackNCrackBB. He was greeted with a new communication from his benefactor, which he immediately decrypted.

*Excellent work yesterday. New request, due tonight. Behind the scenes at* Carousel of Progress. *Backstage entry and location of all machinery, especially hydraulics, with extra focus on the Christmas scene.*

Habst wrote back, encrypting his message before sending it.

*No can do. Got banned yesterday. Trespassing charge if caught on property again. Not worth the risk. Sorry. It's been a good run.*

Within seconds, another message came in.

*We'll make it worth the risk. 10 VTC. If you get arrested, your bail will be paid.*

"Holy crap!" said Habst. 10 VTC was over a thousand dollars. For a single video!

*You got a deal! But I don't want to post it on my public channel. That's just asking for trouble.*

*Do you think they're on to our arrangement?*

Habst paused, and considered this. If he posted another

video, Charlie might assume that he'd been back in the park. But there's no way he could figure out that Habst was being paid to shoot these…. Or could he?

*I doubt it. But Charlie Walker is one smart detective. He'll definitely be watching to see if I post more videos. Will he figure out the connection? Possibly. Best not to risk it.*

*Okay. We'll create a bogus account under the username DisGeek1966. Add that account to the video's access list. If all goes well, we'll have huge job for you in a few days. Keep checking your messages.*

*10-4. Expect the vid to be uploaded tonight.*

He logged out of the site, undocked his laptop, grabbed his backpack, and headed upstairs to retrieve his phone. Dropping the backpack on the floor of the main landing, he walked up the grand staircase to Monika's bedroom. He opened the door slowly, wincing as it creaked. Tiptoeing to the bed, he slowly lifted his phone off the nightstand, which was inconveniently located right next to Monika's face.

"Habst, what are you doing?"

"Damn."

Monika sat up, rubbing her eyes. She scowled.

"Were you going on a Disney adventure without me?"

Habst shrugged.

"Reginald Habstermeister, how dare you?!"

She jumped out of the bed and ran over to him.

"You fucking asshole! You promised!"

She slapped him across the face.

"Ow!" he said, rubbing his face. "I don't need you drawing attention to me! I just need to get in, do the job, and get out."

"Nuh uh. Nope. I'm coming with you. I'll be ready in five minutes. Don't move."

"But, Monika!"

"Don't you dare move, Habst!"

Thirty minutes later, Monika emerged from the bathroom, dressed like a stripper. She was wearing a white cotton button-up shirt with no bra, a short plaid schoolgirl skirt, knee-high knit stockings, and three-inch heels.

"Oh, for Christ's sake! You're going to stand out like a black person at a John Mayer concert!"

"That's racist. And good, I want to stand out. I'm your distraction, remember?"

"Oh yeah…. Right."

"So we'll go in separately. As you're going through the bag check and the main gate I'll do something to distract everyone."

"Okay… that actually sounds like a good plan. Weird."

"Aw, you're so cute when you're being a condescending jerk." She slapped him again, hard enough to bring a tear to his eye.

"Goddammit!"

She smiled sweetly and rubbed his cheek.

"So what's the mission today?"

"The mission is for you to stop slapping me!"

She pulled her hand back again and he winced.

"Okay, okay! Please, stop!" He took a step back and put his arms up in a boxing stance. "I have no problem hitting a girl."

"Try it. My nose alone is insured for a million dollars. They'll lock you up and throw away the key."

"Fine, whatever. Just stop slapping me already! Truce?"

"Truce."

He put his guard down.

"Okay. The mission is to go backstage at *Carousel of Progress*, film the stuff that makes the animatronics move, and then upload the video to YouTube."

"Oooh, sounds dangerous. I'm already getting wet."

"This is serious business, Monika! If I get caught, they'll throw me in jail. For a long time. Charlie was pissed yesterday, and I don't think he's kidding around."

"I'm sure I could convince Charlie not to turn you over to the police," she said, pushing her breasts together.

"I seriously doubt that. Charlie is the most devoted husband ever. Guy would do anything for his family. He's a good dude. I kinda feel bad that I keep messing with him."

"Well, then we'll just have to be sure he doesn't find out you're there."

"Yeah…."

"So let's get moving already!"

Habst didn't move. He was trying to figure something out.

"What's the problem?" asked Monika.

"So… you don't have a fake Cast Member ID?"

"No, of course not. Can you get me one?!"

Habst continued, ignoring her question.

"So… we can't take the Cast Member bus into the Utilidors."

"No, apparently not."

"So… we'll have to go in through the main gate?"

"That's the plan."

"And pay for tickets?!"

"Yes, Habst, we'll have to go in through the main gate and pay for tickets, just like normal people."

"Wow. I haven't done that since like… forever!" He paused. "Uh, Monika?"

"Yes?"

"You think you can spot me for the ticket? I'm pretty sure they're really expensive these days. If I have to pay for it, that kinda defeats the purpose of taking the job, you know? I mean, if I wasn't with you, I'd just go on the bus, but since I'm with you and have to go through the main gate, I kinda…."

She cut him off.

"Yes, fine, Habst. I'll pay for your ticket. Can we leave now?"

He nodded, and they walked downstairs together, only to be stopped at the landing by Ms. Purcelli.

"And where do you think you two are going?"

"Uh… The Most Magical Place on Earth?" replied Habst.

Ms. Purcelli shot him a look of pure hatred.

He smiled weakly.

"Monika," she said, turning to her daughter. "You have a photo shoot for a *Seventeen* fashion spread today. So trouncing around Disneyland is out of the question."

"It's not Disneyland," said Habst.

"Shut up," said Ms. Purcelli. "You're on thin ice, mister."

"Shit, that's right," said Monika. "I totally forgot about the shoot."

Ms. Purcelli nodded smugly.

"So get back upstairs, deslutify yourself, and get ready to leave. We're supposed to be there in an hour." She turned to Habst, and waved a stack of papers in his face. "And while she's getting ready, you and I are going to talk about these astronomical electric bills! Your stupid computers are putting us in the poorhouse!"

"Ask Mr. Purcelli to up the alimony."

"I've already done that. Twice."

"Have you tried banging his lawyer?"

"How do you think I got the last increase?"

"Gross," said Monika. "You know what, Mom? Fuck it. Reschedule it. Or cancel it. I don't care. I'm going on an adventure with Habst!"

Monika grabbed his arm, and they ran out the door together. Habst got into the passenger seat of her ridiculously expensive Beamer.

"Monika, get back here!" screamed Ms. Purcelli. "We need this job!"

"Bye, Mom!" shouted Monika as she peeled out of the driveway.

"Bye, Ms. Purcelli!" said Habst, waving.

"Goddamn you, Reginald! This is the last straw!"

Ms. Purcelli's curses faded as they sped away. Habst pulled his pipe out of the front pocket of his backpack, packed it with Blueberry Cheese, lit it, and pulled down a hit. He offered it to Monika, who also took a hit.

Habst relaxed.

"This might actually be fun," he said.

# TEN

HABST HAD MET MONIKA on his last day at Custodial. It was a Friday night during the annual Food and Wine Festival, and the locals were out in full force. Epcot was already notorious for drunken Guest shenanigans, including the much maligned "Drink Around the World" challenge. But Food and Wine tripled the amount of booze offerings in the park, inevitably leading to copious overconsumption, especially by local Annual Passholders who used Epcot as their neighborhood bar. Every Friday they'd get off work, drive to Epcot, get shitfaced, piss or puke in a bush, and pass out on a bench.

It was not a fun time to be a janitor in Epcot. Habst hated cleaning up bodily fluids, but he was used to it. Little kids shit, pissed, and puked everywhere, all day long. What he never got used to, though, was the awful behavior of drunken adults. Every weekend was an unending series of fights, destruction of property, and defecation in and around every trash can and piece of foliage in the park. He'd even heard of people caught having sex in public.

The worst thing was that this all took place in full view of children. Children brought to the park for a wholesome vacation by parents clueless about the annual debauchery caused by Food and Wine.

Habst was pretty sure that this was not Walt's vision of what an Experimental Prototype Community of Tomorrow was supposed to look like.

So he was in no mood for someone like Monika that evening. Monika was pretty much the epitome of all he hated about the typical Food and Wine female Guest: scantily dressed, stupidly drunk, and acting like a complete and total slut.

He first saw her in Japan, doing saké shots with two 'roided out frat boy jocks wearing tattered baseball caps, polo shirts with popped collars, khaki shorts, and sandals. He didn't drink, but he knew that saké was best when sipped and savored. The traditionally dressed Japanese hostess behind the bar tried to explain this to Monika and her friends, but they just laughed at her, made fun of her accent, threw money at her face, and stumbled out onto the central walkway.

The scene enraged Habst so much that he didn't even notice Monika was easily the hottest girl he'd ever seen in person.

"Fuck this foreign shit," yelled Jock #1. "I want some goddamned good old refreshing American beer!"

"'Merica!" roared Jock #2.

They turned right and headed towards The American Adventure. Habst followed, pushing along his mop and bucket, knowing from years of experience that within minutes he'd be cleaning up some sort of mess from these idiots.

Monika and the meatheads stopped at the Sam Adams booth across from the American Gardens stage and tried to order Bud Lights. When the Cast Member at the podium told them they didn't serve Bud Light, the jocks started yelling at her. She deftly convinced them that Boston Lager tasted just like Bud Light, so all three ordered twenty-two-ounce collectible mugs of Boston Lager. The two idiot jocks dared each other to chug their entire mug, which they both did, as

Monika applauded and squealed.

Night Ranger was playing at the American Gardens stage that night. Habst loved Night Ranger. In his mind, Brad Gillis was one of the best guitarists ever, and Jack Blades was one of the best frontmen ever. The fact that they were only given thirty-minute sets was a disservice to their epic back catalog, but Habst understood that logistics necessitated the shitty schedule. The auditorium wasn't that big, so the bands had to play three short sets in order to accommodate everyone who might want to see them that evening.

"You suck!" yelled Jock #1, pointing at the theater as the band ended their set with their classic hit (*You Can Still) Rock in America*.

"'Merica!" yelled Jock #2.

"Wooooo!" yelled Monika, raising her beer above her head, spilling half of it on the ground, and then lowering the mug and gulping down the rest.

They doubled back, either forgetting or not caring that they'd just come from that direction. They passed Japan and entered the Morocco pavilion.

Habst followed, keeping a safe distance.

"Monika, what the fuck are we doing here?" said Jock #1. "Bunch of goddamned Towel Heads in this place."

"I like their pretty clothes and jewelry," said Monika, picking up a jewel-encrusted purse. "The colors are so beautiful!"

"What, you want to look like a Camel Jockey? Fuckers blew up New York, and now you're trying to look like them?"

"'Merica!" shouted Jock #2 yet again.

"I'm pretty sure Moroccans didn't have anything to do with 9/11," said Monika.

"Whatever," said Jock #1. "They look like a bunch of fucking Derka Derkas to me."

"Yeah," said Jock #2. "Listen to that cashier. 'Derka derka derka derka derka.' Can't understand a fucking thing she's saying."

"They were a French colony," said Monika. "That's a French accent."

"Fucking towel-headed Frogs?!" said Jock #1. "That's even worse! Let's get the fuck out of here!"

Monika shook her head.

"Okay, I'm not buying anything," she said, putting down the purse. "Can we at least get something to drink?"

"Here?!" said Jock #1. "Are you trying to get us poisoned?"

"I don't want to be poisoned!" said Jock #2.

"Yeah, I'm not drinking shit from these Sand Monkeys!" said Jock #1. "Probably serve us camel piss with anthrax in it or something."

"Ugh, fine!" said Monika, storming out of the pavilion.

"What's got her panties in a bunch?" asked Jock #2.

"Dunno. Probably... my cock!" said Jock #1.

They both laughed, high-fived each other, and followed Monika back out to the main walkway.

"What a bunch of idiots," said Habst, as he continued following them.

Torches in front of each World Showcase pavilion burned as the rest of the lights around the lagoon dimmed. The nightly show, *IllumiNations*, was beginning.

"Good evening," said a voice over speakers hidden around the lagoon. "On behalf of Walt Disney World, the place where dreams come true, we welcome all of you to Epcot and World Showcase."

Monika stood at a booth across from the France pavilion.

"Grey Goose Slushie, please," she said, and swiped her credit card.

A Cast Member handed her a cup of the frozen alcoholic beverage, and Monika stepped away from the booth.

There was a sound of a flame being blown out, and all of the torches extinguished, plunging the entire World Showcase into darkness.

"Monika, where the fuck are you?" yelled Jock #1.

Monika stepped forward, disoriented by the darkness.

"Over here!" she yelled.

"Over where, dammit?!"

She turned towards his voice, tripped on the cobblestone pavement, and launched her Grey Goose Slush through the air. It landed directly onto Jock #1's head.

The drink saturated his baseball cap and splashed onto his pink polo.

"What the fuck?!" he yelled, enraged.

"Oh my god, I'm so sorry!" said Monika, rushing up to him.

Without hesitating, Jock #1 pivoted sharply and planted a hard left hook onto the side of Monika's chin. She crumbled.

"Oh shit!" said Habst.

"Goddamn!" yelled Jock #2. "That was some hardcore MMA action right there!"

"That bitch spilled a Slurpee on my lid!" slurred Jock #1, shaking out his baseball cap.

"Total bullshit, man. I mean, that's your favorite lid!"

The two looked down at Monika, as explosions and flames emanated from the center of the lagoon.

"Fuckin' bitch," said Jock #1. "Thinks she can just go around ruining my favorite lid. Hell no! Pick her up. Bitch is gonna pay."

"Fucking A right!" roared Jock #2. He picked her up and slung her over his shoulder. The two walked through the crowd, who, captivated by *IllumiNations*, didn't give them a second glance.

"Are you kidding me?" said Habst. "Who acts like this?!"

He pulled his radio out of the holster on his belt.

"Sam 12, we have a situation in World Showcase. 10-45, Code... uh... Code 2, I guess. 514 two large males carrying an unconscious female towards Morocco."

"10-4," said the voice on the other end of the radio.

"Okay.... And? Should I follow them?"

"Negative. Sam 12 will handle it."

Habst watched as the meatheads entered the Morocco pavilion. Jock #1 pointed to the pavilion's Companion Restroom, one of the few publicly accessible places in the park with a door that locked from the inside. Jock #2 nodded, and they went into the restroom. Monika was still unconscious, and blood was dripping from her mouth.

"What's the ETA on Sam 12?"

"Right now?" The voice on the other end of the radio sighed. "ETA ten minutes? It's a mess tonight."

"Crap," said Habst. "Sam 12, ten minutes isn't going to cut it. They've… uh… it's a Code… uh…. You know what? I don't know the goddamned code. There are two drunken jerks who knocked a girl out. They just took her into the Morocco Companion Restroom. Permission to engage?"

"Permission denied. Wait for Sam 12."

"She'll be raped and maybe even dead in ten minutes."

"Repeat: wait for Sam 12. Do not engage!"

"Piss off," said Habst.

He holstered the radio, pulled out his chain of keys, found the master key for the Companion Restrooms, and approached the door, pushing his mop and bucket in front of him.

Reaching the restroom door, he thought he could hear the jocks yelling, but he couldn't make out what they were saying over the din of the fireworks echoing across the lagoon. But in his mind, it sounded like the scumbags were already tag-teaming her and roaring it up.

Habst hadn't been in a fight in his life. He'd been a downright coward, in fact. But he knew he couldn't sit back and let this happen, even if it did mean getting the crap beat out of him. At the very least, he could try to put up a decent fight, so that by the time the meatheads were done kicking his ass and were ready to move back to the girl, Security would have shown up.

He quietly unlocked the door, slowly pulled the key out of the lock, and then started preparing for battle. He knew that he had no chance against these guys if he fought fairly. So he decided to fight as dirty as possible. He sorted through the keychain, found the longest, sharpest-looking key, and clenched it between the fingers of his right hand so that the pointed and jagged end of the key stuck out from his fist. With the other hand, he pulled his mop out of his bucket, grasped it midway down the handle, and wedged the end of it into his armpit, as if preparing to joust.

"Okay, here we go."

With his right hand, he slowly turned the handle, cracked the door open, and re-clenched his fist onto the key. Then he stuck his right foot into the crack and used his leg to fling the door open.

"Aaaahhhhhh!!!" he yelled, storming into the bathroom, broom and key-hand raised for battle.

Monika was standing in the middle of the room, holding a canister of pepper spray. The two meatheads lay on the floor, squirming in pain. Jock #1's shorts and boxers were down around his ankles.

Habst stopped, stared at the jocks for a second, and then looked up at Monika, his mouth agape.

She shrugged.

"Uh…," he said.

"My knight in shining armor, I presume?"

"Uh, I mean, I just…."

"Aw, you're cute. Really cute, actually. I'm fine, though. But since you went through all the trouble to prep for battle, you wanna take a shot at one of these assholes?"

Habst shook his head.

"Okay, more fun for me, then!" said Monika.

She kicked Jock #1 in the stomach, laughed, and emptied the bottle of pepper spray onto his penis and testicles. He screamed in agony.

Only then did Habst realize that Monika was easily the hottest girl he'd ever seen in person.

---

LATER THAT NIGHT, he was fired for disobeying direct orders. Charlie went to bat for him, but it was no use. Habst's supervisor had wanted him gone since his first day on the job, and this was a perfect excuse to give him the boot.

Habst was already three months late on his rent. So, the next day, knowing he wouldn't be able to square up with his landlord without a job, Habst skipped out on his lease and moved into Monika's house. He thought it would only be temporary, but it turned out Monika had a thing for loveable losers. Or at least that's what she told him. He had a sneaking suspicion that she had daddy issues, and only dated men who were bad for her. But free rent was free rent, so he didn't ask questions.

A week later, after they'd had sex dozens of times, he learned she was only sixteen.

But, by then, it was too late. Habst was hooked on Monika Purcelli, and on the decadent, carefree lifestyle she provided for him.

# ELEVEN

PER HABST'S DIRECTIONS, Monika sped down the back roads leading to the Magic Kingdom's parking lot, avoiding the parking fee.

"I could've just paid the seventeen dollars, you know," said Monika.

"Eh, we actually would've had to go out of our way to get through the booths. Plus, seventeen bucks for parking is ridiculous. I can't support that nonsense."

They parked in the Cruella section of the lot, and hopped on the "Villains" tram.

"This is awesome," said Habst. "I haven't been on one of these trams since I was a kid. Plus, Cruella looks like your mom!"

Monika punched him on the shoulder, and a few minutes later, the tram dropped them off at the ticket booths.

"Two adults please," said Monika to the attendant at the ticket booth.

"That'll be two hundred and ten dollars and eighty-eight cents."

"Holy shit, are you kidding me?!" yelled Habst.

"Calm down," said Monika. She turned and smiled at the ticket booth attendant.

"That's completely insane!" continued Habst. "Who the hell can afford that?! Walt wanted parks that everyone could enjoy, and you've just priced out ninety-five percent of the population! How do you live with yourself?!"

Monika turned to Habst, grabbed his crotch, and squeezed.

"You're making a scene. Stop. Now."

"Yes, ma'am," said Habst, grimacing.

Monika released her grip on Habst's crotch, turned back to the ticket attendant, and handed her two hundreds and a twenty.

"Here's your change and your tickets. Have a magical day!" said the attendant.

"Thank you," said Monika.

They turned away from the ticket booth, and Monika glared at him.

"What?!" he asked.

"If you wanted to remain inconspicuous, you're not off to a good start."

"I can't help it. That's total bullshit!"

"Well, you didn't pay for it. I did. So shut up and try to look like a tourist."

"You shut up," said Habst.

"Excuse me?"

"Nothing."

"That's what I thought."

They boarded the monorail to the main gate, and had the car all to themselves. Monika started groping Habst.

"Cut it out, woman!"

"C'mon, Habst, just a quickie?"

"No!"

"Please?"

"NO!"

"Ugh, you're no fun," she said, plopping down onto the padded aquamarine seat.

"Now you're the one putting the job in jeopardy," said

Habst. "We're here on business. Business first, pleasure later."

"You promise?"

"Promise what?"

"Pleasure later?"

"Uh, sure. I promise."

Monika bounced, her breasts jiggling rhythmically.

"I definitely promise," said Habst, mesmerized.

The monorail pulled into the station at the main gate of the Magic Kingdom. Habst and Monika exited and started walking down the ramp.

"Let me go through bag check first," said Monika. "When they're distracted, you go through."

"Uh, okay…. This is never going to work, you know."

"Just you watch."

Monika walked up to the bag check area, spotted the youngest male guard, and went into his lane. She handed over her purse, smiled as the guard stared at her breasts while pretending to sort through her bag, and walked away with an innocent "Bye!"

She took a few steps towards the turnstiles and promptly spilled the entire contents of her bag all over the ground. Bending over, she revealed a bright-pink thong under her skirt.

The bag check guard, completely against protocol, rushed to help her gather her belongings back into her purse.

Habst stared at the scene, slack jawed. She glanced back at him, smiled, and said, "Oh my, I don't know why I decided to bring my vibrator with me today."

"Holy shit," said Habst.

He walked casually through a bag check line. None of the guards gave him a second look. He chose the closest turnstile to the bag check that was staffed by a young male Cast Member, held his ticket against the RFID reader, pressed his finger on the biometric scanner, and went through the turnstile. The Cast Member never even looked at him. He was entirely fixated on Monika, who was bent over, stuffing a long string of condoms back into her purse.

"Well I'll be damned," said Habst.

He walked under the Railroad station archway, out onto Main Street, and made a beeline for Tomorrowland. He ducked into *Monsters, Inc. Laugh Floor* and texted Monika, letting her know where he was. And then, he waited.

The show finished. He was ushered out of the theater. He looped back in. Another show finished. He felt like he was starting to look suspicious. Nobody saw the *Laugh Floor* more than once. Nobody.

He left the theater and aimlessly wandered over to *Stitch's Great Escape*, only to find a sign on the door that said, "This Area Is Being Refurbished For Your Future Enjoyment." That was odd. He'd been in there the day before, and everything was fine. The show had sucked, but nothing was broken.

He went over to the bathrooms in the Tomorrowland Terrace. The place was shuttered most of the year, so the bathrooms were always deserted. As a result, they also happened to be the cleanest restrooms in the park.

Habst went into a stall and sat on the toilet, on the off chance he might actually be able to take a dump, and texted Monika again.

*In the bathroom at Tomorrowland Terrace. Where are you?!*

No response. Now he was getting worried.

Ten minutes later, Habst was still sitting on the throne, unable to have a bowel movement, when someone ran into the bathroom, talking loudly.

"Join me... shall you? For a tour of the best bathroom... in the Magic Kingdom!"

Habst sighed, got off the toilet, pulled his pants up, and exited the stall.

"Seriously, dude?" said Habst, heading to the sink and shaking his head at a bearded man with large white sunglasses and a video camera.

"Look, everyone, it's a man! An angry man. In the bathroom! In the best men's bathroom. Look, everyone, it's an angry man in the best Men's bathroom!" yelled the videographer.

"Very cute," said Habst, washing his hands. "Nice schtick. Send me the link when you put this on YouTube. My username is DisneyHabst."

The bearded videographer slowly lowered his camera.

"Holy cow, you're DisneyHabst?"

"In the flesh, man."

"Wow, dude, awesome! You're like… you're like Mr. Bigtime! You have over a hundred thousand subscribers!"

"Yep."

"Any words of wisdom for everyone out there in YouTubeLand? You know, the viewers? The people? Our people?!"

"Uh… You know, just, uh, keep doing your thing. Don't listen to the haters. Hard work begets success. Material possessions are overrated. You know, just general crap like that."

"You heard it here first, everyone!" said the man to his camera. "Words of wisdom from the man himself, DisneyHabst! DisneyHabst, everyone! Look, look! It's DisneyHabst!"

Habst waved at the camera, dried his hands, threw the paper towel away, and walked out of the bathroom.

Stepping out into the harsh sunlight, he looked back and forth between Main Street and Tomorrowland. At this point he was pretty sure that either Charlie had figured everything out and had apprehended Monika, or that she had chickened out and gone home. He didn't know whether to continue on with the job or not. So he just stood there, frozen with indecision. Should he try to get out of the park unnoticed as quickly as possible? Should he continue on to *Carousel* and hopefully get his 10 VTC without getting caught? It was a lot of money. He could massively upgrade his mining rig and still have enough leftover for an ounce of that Pineapple Express that his favorite vendor had just listed.

The thought of vaping some Pineapple Express made him salivate.

"Well, that seals it, then," he said, turning to leave the Tomorrowland Terrace.

"That seals what?" said Monika, grabbing his ass.

Habst spun around.

"Where the hell have you been?!" he yelled. "I was worried sick! I thought you'd been captured, or had wussed out, and I couldn't figure out what to do, and then I wanted to smoke some Pineapple Express, and then…."

"They offered me a job as a princess!" said Monika.

"What?!"

"The second I turn eighteen, they're going to hire me to play Snow White! They said I have beautiful skin."

"What the hell are you talking about? Where were you? What happened?!"

"Well, I was walking through the turnstiles, and I guess a Casting Manager must have noticed how much attention I was getting from the male Cast Members and all of the fathers in line. So he pulled me aside and offered me a job right there, on the spot. Didn't even need to audition!"

"Wait, did you actually say you'd take the job?!"

"Of course I did! It's every girl's dream to be a princess. And Snow White is the best princess of them all!"

She spun around, grinning from ear to ear.

"I'm Snow White! I'm Snow White!"

"But that's ridiculous," said Habst. "The face characters get paid like fourteen bucks an hour. You make at least five hundred for a one-hour photo shoot!"

"Yeah, but I don't like doing photo shoots. Fuck photo shoots. I want to be a princess! Stop being a buzzkill and be happy for me, Habst!"

"Your mom is going to kill me. She's going to have to switch from Johnnie Walker Blue Label to Black Label. That's going to make her cranky as all getout."

"Whatever, Habst. I don't care. I'm Snow White!"

She started twirling again. He stared at her, mouth agape. But then a smile slowly crept across his face. Her joy was infectious. He grabbed her arm, pulled her against him, and kissed her.

"You'll make a wonderful Snow White," he said. "I'm very proud of you. Now can we get this job over with and get out of here before Charlie finds out I'm here?"

Monika wiped a tear from her eye, kissed him back, grabbed his hand, and started skipping towards the *Carousel of Progress*.

"I'm a princess, I'm Snow White, I'm a princess!" she sang over and over.

Habst smiled. She was a real trip.

# TWELVE

CONTINUED FROM PAGE 13

Satoru was, according to experts, merely a passable software programmer. His code was elegant at times, but usually no more than utilitarian. However, what he lacked in coding expertise, he made up for with a vast knowledge and passion for the disparate fields of cryptography, economics, and peer-to-peer networking. And the true genius of his creation was in how he combined these unique disciplines in a creative and entirely revolutionary manner. Oblivious to years of struggle by the cypherpunks to create a viable cryptocurrency, Satoru was single-handedly able to not only create Virtcoin, but to put it into public circulation by appealing to the needs of computer geeks, libertarians, and criminals.

Of course, this didn't all happen at once. Satoru claimed to have started work on the virtcoin protocol in 2007. On Saturday, November 1, 2008, he published an overview of the currency on an obscure cypherpunk online mailing list. Given that he was a relative unknown and hadn't made any previous contributions of any significance, his post was looked at as a bit of a joke. The only person to comment on the paper that day said it was "naively implemented" and "[did] not seem to scale to the required size".

Despite the lack of enthusiasm, on Friday, January 9, 2009, Satoru released a fully functional software package that created the currency's underlying peer-to-peer network. Satoru then used the network to mine the first batch of fifty virtcoins, which are now known as the Singularity Block.

News of the software's simplicity and ease of use quickly spread throughout the online tech community, and within a year the value of the currency surpassed the symbolically important exchange rate of 1 VTC per 1 USD, aka "dollar parity".

But then, just as his currency was achieving critical mass, something totally unexpected happened: Satoru vanished.

Initially, he'd been fairly involved in refining and debugging the virtcoin protocol. He'd actively posted technical information about the software on semiofficial message boards, and modified and rereleased the source code often. It seemed as if he was in it for the long-haul. After all, as one of the first adopters of the currency, he'd mined a significant number of virtcoins himself (it has been estimated that Satoru still holds 1.2 million VTC, currently worth $156 million), and thus had a vested interest in seeing the value of the currency continue to increase.

However, near the end of 2010, Satoru's updates to the online community slowed to a crawl. His last forum post was on Sunday, December 12. In one of his final posts, when questioned about his lack of updates, his only response was, "I've moved on to other things."

Then, on Tuesday, April 26, 2011, Satoru sent an email to developer Gareth Pedersen, one of the few people who Satoru trusted to help him improve the core virtcoin code. In this email, Satoru named Pedersen as his successor, and gave him a copy of the Alert Key, a secret code used to notify users of any issues within the virtcoin network.

The following day, Pedersen announced that he was

going to meet with the CIA to "give a presentation about Virtcoin... at an emerging technologies conference for the US intelligence community." There was obvious skepticism about his motives, and it is highly doubtful that Satoru believed him. Either way, Satoru would have certainly felt betrayed. The day after handing the reins over to his chosen successor, that successor announced a meeting with the CIA. The timing was certainly suspicious.

The April 26 email was the last time Satoru communicated with Pedersen. It was, in fact, the last time he communicated with anyone. After that email, he simply fell off the face of the earth.

One thing became clear in the aftermath of Satoru Kobayashi's disappearance: he was, and had always been, a total cipher. Satoru Kobayashi had never really existed. His name returned no Google search results pre-2008. His domain name registration information was hidden by a privacy service. His email address belonged to a German ISP, yet his forum profiles listed his location as Japan. He wrote in perfect English, but often switched between British and American spellings.

Some have speculated that Satoru was never just one person, but maybe a group of multiple software developers, retaining their anonymity by hiding behind a fictitious persona. Yet everyone involved in the development of Virtcoin denies this, and all have plausible alibis. Others have suggested that he was a creation of the CIA, who were looking to smoke out money launderers. Or a front for a major financial institution, running a long con, like a global pyramid scheme. Some even claimed he was Julian Assange, the founder of WikiLeaks. Others have speculated that Satoru died in Japan's 2011 tsunami, although the timeline doesn't quite line up.

But Occam's razor tells us that Satoru Kobayashi was in all likelihood a lone, brilliant individual who was in the right place at the right time. The simplest explanations are usually the correct ones.

But none of the speculation matters, because Satoru is now the stuff of legend. He is a cyberhero. "I AM SATORU" t-shirts can be seen at tech conventions, stretched tightly across hairy overweight bellies and model-perfect double-D breasts alike. And his currency thrives, used millions of times daily by everyone from the heads of Al Qaeda to pot-smoking college kids. Satoru's legacy has yet to be written, but there are many people, this author included, who are certain that his name will be entered in the history books as one of the most influential figures of the twenty-first century.

# THIRTEEN

**H**ABST AND MONIKA SKIPPED over to the *Carousel of Progress*, holding hands and smiling like little kids.

When they got close to the entrance ramp, Habst realized that he had no plan to get around to the back of the building without being noticed. The Cast Member at the greeting station could easily see anyone trying to sneak under the chains cordoning off the back of the building. The whole plan might be DOA.

"Oh, that poor little girl," said Monika, pointing.

Habst turned to her, confused.

"What?"

"That little girl's father just slapped her, told her to stop crying, and then threw her Mouse Ears into the trash can! What an asshole!"

"That's really sad and all, Monika, but I'm trying to figure out some way to get backstage without being seen, and I can't really be concerned about...."

She ignored him and walked towards the *Carousel of Progress*, still staring at the man who had slapped his daughter.

"Okay... so I guess I'll just wait here and try to think of something, then?" asked Habst.

Monika approached the female Cast Member at the

greeting station, whispered something into her ear, and pointed at the abusive father, who was entering a Companion Restroom next to Space Mountain with his daughter. The Cast Member gasped, grabbed her radio, and ran towards the man, yelling, "Sam 12, we have a situation! Need all the dwarfs you've got for a 514!"

Habst ran up to Monika, who was standing at the top of the *Carousel* ramp, smiling smugly.

"Holy shit, Monika, what the hell was that all about?"

"I told her that I was an off-duty Cast Member, and that I'd just seen that man slap his daughter and then put his hand down her pants and fondle her."

"What?!"

"Security will be dealing with that situation for a while. Let's get moving before the CM comes back to her station."

Habst shook his head in disbelief as he watched the Cast Member point at the restroom and whisper into Smelly's ear. Smelly quickly pulled a key out of his pocket, opened the door, and stood aside as Angry pulled the father out of the restroom and threw him on the ground. Angry, Smelly, and the father were immediately surrounded by ten other security guards, who formed a circle around them. The last thing Habst saw before the circle cut off his view was Angry and Smelly repeatedly punching and kicking the father.

"Wow, I just… wow. You are one crazy bitch. Remind me never to cross you again."

"Never cross me again, Habst!" she yelled, smacking his ass. "Now lead the way, my fearless explorer." She hooked her arm through his. "Adventure awaits around every corner!"

"Yeah… sure," said Habst, tearing his gaze from the scene of havoc his girlfriend had caused. "I guess we should get going.…"

Habst put his fake ID around his neck, pulled out his phone, checked the settings, and started recording. He pointed the camera at Monika, who blew a kiss at it and flashed her tits.

"Nice," said Habst. "Maybe I'll get an extra virtcoin for those."

They ducked under the chains and made their way down the walkway until they reached two black doors a full one hundred and eighty degrees from the main entrance of the ride. They were now hidden from view, at least from anyone in the park.

Monika opened one of the doors, which led to a concrete ramp. They both walked down the ramp and into a small circular hallway that wrapped around the core of the building. Throughout the hallway were doors that led to rooms directly under the stages. They opened the first door, entered a pie-slice-shaped room, and heard the show going on above them. John, the patriarch of the family, talked about the rat race, and his daughter Patty was trying to lose weight while blabbing to Babs about her dreamboat date. Massive motors on either side of the room powered turntables that rotated to reveal different characters over the course of the scene.

Habst walked towards the outer edge of the building and yanked at a door labeled "Machinery Room". The door wouldn't budge.

"It's locked," said Habst, jiggling the knob. "This sucks. I'm supposed to film this stuff."

"Move out of the way," said Monika. "You're useless."

She pulled a bobby pin and a small flathead screwdriver out of her purse, stuck the pin into the lock, put the end of the flathead in the bottom of the lock, turned it to apply pressure, and raked the pin back and forth. After a few seconds, the lock clicked. She rotated the flathead clockwise and opened the door.

"That was maybe the hottest thing I've ever seen any woman do," said Habst.

"Well, it's a skill you learn pretty quickly when you want to party, but your bitch of a mother has locked you in your bedroom for the night."

They walked down a dark path under the theater's seating area, and into a small room. Inside the dingy, dirty alcove were mechanisms that controlled the movement of the main turntable. As the theater rotated, Habst shot close-ups of the main motor and all of the pulleys, gears, and chains that worked together to move the audience from scene to scene. He couldn't even begin to imagine what sort of power was needed to move six theaters full of people around that central shaft, but the motor was huge, and it was noisy.

"I love heavy machinery," said Monika

She pressed herself against the wall directly under the motor and moaned.

"Habst, it's like the most powerful vibrator ever!"

"Get away from that!"

"Uhhhhh," she said, her voice modulating with the rhythm of the motor.

"C'mon!" said Habst, trying to pull her away.

The motor stopped, and a large glob of grease fell onto his head.

"What the hell?"

He touched the top of his head and then looked at his hand. It was covered in jet-black lubricant.

"Serves you right," said Monika. "Trying to stop me from getting off. Asshole."

"Getting you off is my job, dammit!"

"The motor does it better."

"You've never complained before."

"I've never had a thousand-watt vibrator before. You know what they say, 'Once you go *Carousel of Progress* turntable motor, you never go back.'"

"That doesn't even rhyme."

"You don't even rhyme."

"What? Shut up. Help me get this crap off my head!"

She looked around and found a dirty shop rag on the floor.

She picked it up with her fingertips, held it at arms length, and handed it to Habst. It was stiff.

"Gross," he said.

He dabbed his head with it, realized he was just getting his hair even dirtier, and threw it on the ground.

"Screw it," he said, running his hands through his hair and slicking it back.

"You look like Ronald Reagan," said Monika.

"Ronald Reagan?"

"Yeah. Your hair is all black and slicked back. It's sexy."

"You're seventeen. How the hell do you even know what Ronald Reagan looks like?"

"*Hall of Presidents*? Duh. I gave a guy a blowjob in there a few years back, and ever since then I've had a thing for Reagan."

"Give me a goddamned break." He wiped his hands on his jeans. "Let's go."

They exited the machinery room, went back down to the circular hallway, and walked counterclockwise to the next room. Upon opening the door, they heard two 8mm projectors whirring away. Lying on the floor was a huge box full of broken and split filmstrips. Monika pulled one strip out of the box and held it up to the light.

"Hey," said Monika, "it's the boxing match that Grandma is watching in the Halloween scene!"

"Cool," said Habst, shoving the filmstrip into his backpack.

Moving to the next room, Habst could hear Grandma winning at a virtual reality space pilot game directly above them. He turned the camera upward, and filmed the pumps, fluid lines, valves, and filters that controlled the motion of the animatronic figures above. Thick steel plates were bolted to the ceiling where the figures were mounted. Small stress cracks spread from each plate, but the damage to the concrete didn't seem to be significant.

They walked to the next room, which was much darker

than the others. Habst pulled a flashlight from his backpack and turned it on, pointing it towards the wall.

Monika screamed.

The flashlight illuminated a severed animatronic head. It was Sarah, the mother of the show, hairless, with her eyes gouged out and the skin of her left cheek torn and hanging grotesquely over her mouth. As Habst moved the flashlight around they saw shelves filled with spools of wire, crusty pumps and split valves, and entire animatronic bodies, stripped of their skin, missing various body parts, and contorted into disturbing positions.

"This is creepy as hell," said Habst, filming the whole thing.

"I'm freaking out, Habst. Can we get out of here? Like, now?!"

They went back to the hallway, and Habst pointed to a stairway in the center core, opposite the rooms they'd been exploring.

"There," he said, pointing to the stairs. "We have to go up, shoot the backside of the Christmas stage, and get some different angles of the figures. Then we can get out of here."

Monika nodded.

"Ladies first," said Habst, motioning to the steep stairway.

Monika started climbing. Habst filmed her going up a few stairs, and then followed, positioning the camera so it shot up her skirt. He stopped climbing and zoomed into her pink thong, which fell a few millimeters short of covering what it was made to cover.

"I'm gonna get so much Google ad revenue from this if I ever make it public," said Habst.

Monika looked down, saw what he was doing, and instinctively kicked him in the face. He fell backward, tumbled down the stairs, and landed on the concrete floor.

"Ouch."

Monika finished climbing the stairs and looked down at him.

"Is your phone okay?" she asked.

"My phone?"

"Stop being such a pussy, Habst. Are you still recording?"

Habst lifted his hand, checked the phone, and verified that it was indeed still recording.

"It's okay. It's still filming."

"Good," said Monika. "Then quit perving around and get your ass up here."

Habst sat up and groaned.

"I'm okay, by the way. Thanks for asking. I'm fine. My nuts are halfway up my ass, but other than that, I'm perfect."

He stood, stretched, and felt and heard what he assumed was a disc slipping back into place. He groaned and climbed up the steps, which opened into a large circular room, sparsely lit by cheap fluorescent overhead lights. He could see small sections of each of the turntable sets, flanked by scrims and dark wooden flats which made up the backside of their backdrops.

Monika opened a door and disappeared behind one of the flats. Habst followed. He looked to his left, and saw her standing midway across the backdrop.

"Come over here, and then look around this corner very slowly," she said, pointing forward.

He did as instructed, and found himself looking straight at the faces of at least a dozen people sitting in the Carousel Theater. He yanked his head back, surprised.

Monika giggled.

Habst looked around. Apparently, they were behind the kitchen in the Christmas scene.

"Jackpot," he said.

He positioned the camera just over the window ledge to the right of the John animatronic, and slowly panned it around from one end of the set to the other.

He pulled the camera back, looked to his left, and saw that the walkway between the set and the backdrop curved around the corner.

He motioned to Monika to follow him. She nodded.

Continuing to film, he got on his hands and knees and crawled past the windows. His hands kept pressing into screws, bits of wire, and large chunks of splintered wood. He was glad he was wearing jeans.

He turned the corner, verified that this side of the set was a solid wall with no openings to the audience, and stood up.

Habst looked back to see Monika wincing. Since she'd worn a skirt, her knees were bare, and the trash covering the dirty wooden walkway had cut her up pretty badly.

"This sucks," she said, brushing herself off as she stood up.

"Sorry about that. We're almost done."

He filmed the back of the kitchen set, capturing the pneumatic pump that blew open the oven door when John's voice commands overloaded it. He also filmed the pump and atomizer that produced the smoke that comes from the burned turkey inside the oven.

"Okay, that should be enough," whispered Habst. He stopped recording, uploaded the video to YouTube with the private option selected, added the DisGeek1966 account to the access list, and put his phone away.

"Mission accomplished," said Habst.

He was more relaxed now that his job was done, and was actually getting a little excited about exploring the rest of the sets.

"You up for looking around some more?"

"I guess. Not too much longer, though, okay?" She looked down at her dirty, bloody knees. "I need to get cleaned up. So do you, Mr. President."

"Cut that crap out. Let's just see what's over here, and then we'll leave, okay?"

She nodded, and they crossed over to another stage. Habst opened the door leading to the set, and they stepped into a beautiful backdrop of a sunny outdoor scene, complete with clothes drying on a clothesline.

Unfortunately, once again, there were windows in front of the backdrop, so if they walked a few steps further, the audience would be able to see them.

"Dammit," said Habst.

They doubled back to the main room. Habst looked to his right and pointed.

Uncle Orville himself lay in his bathtub in the rotating side-stage vignette next to them. His skin ended at his torso, which was hidden from the audience by the bathtub. Below the waist Uncle Orville was simply a mess of metal and wires. His skin did resume mid-thigh, although he had a speaker conspicuously placed directly between his legs where his man-bits should have been.

"Poor Uncle Orville is a neuter!" said Monika.

Habst laughed.

"No privacy at all around this place," he said, and kissed her.

Uncle Orville's vignette started to rotate counterclockwise. The small turntable that the set rested on creaked, and Habst could feel the vibration of the powerful motor in the basement as it moved hundreds of pounds of sets and animatronics.

"Here we go!" said Habst, leaning forward and patting Uncle Orville's leg as it passed by. "Orville, buddy, it's your time to shine!"

Monika giggled. Habst ran his fingers through his hair, and kissed her again. The floor continued to vibrate, and he reached out to the wall for support. His greasy hand slipped, and he fell forward, head-butting Monika.

"Oh shit! Sorry!"

She fell backward, and instinctively put her hands behind her to stop her fall. A second after she hit the ground, she started screaming.

Habst looked down and saw that her right hand was caught between the static wall of the main set, and the thick moving partition separating Uncle Orville's scene from Jimmy's scene on the other side of the turntable.

"Habst! It's crushing my wrist!" screamed Monika.

"Holy shit!" yelled Habst.

He thrust his shoulder against the partition and pushed as hard as he could, but it wouldn't budge. The motor was simply too powerful.

Monika screamed even louder as the force of the moving wall broke multiple bones and crushed her radial artery.

A few people in the audience heard the screaming and started looking at each other, wondering if it was rusty machinery, or if they were really hearing someone behind the set.

Habst put his back against the partition and pushed, using every ounce of strength that years of bike riding had given his leg muscles. This stopped it from closing further, but didn't come close to moving it enough for Monika to be able to release her hand. His feet threatened to slide along the wooden floor, and he knew he couldn't keep pushing for much longer. But if he let go, her hand would be severed.

Blood from Monika's artery started shooting rhythmically onto the stage. Someone in the audience saw it, pointed, and screamed. The whole audience started freaking out, and the auditorium quickly turned into complete chaos.

"Somebody help!" yelled Habst through the crack between the partition and the stage wall. "I need some muscle back here! Help! This goddamned thing will cut her hand clean off!"

A small wiry man jumped on the stage, wedged his fingers into the gap between the stage and the base of the partition, and started pulling. The turntable moved a full inch. As astounding as this display of strength was, it didn't create enough of a gap to free Monika's hand, and the loss of pressure on her severed artery made her bleed out even more.

She fainted.

"Monika!" yelled Habst. "Holy shit! Mister! Mister! Help her!"

Habst craned his head sideways and looked pleadingly through the two-inch crack, glimpsing the thin outline of the face of the man on the other side.

He had a long, slim face, a well-manicured moustache, arched eyebrows, and dark, straight hair.

The man looked exactly like a young Walt Disney. Habst was momentarily stunned.

"Wake up, son! We need to coordinate our efforts!" said the man, speaking in a confident, familiar cadence.

"What?!" said Habst.

"Pulling at it won't do a damn thing. Turntable motor's too powerful. We need one quick burst of force to jump the chain from the sprockets. I'll hold it in place. You get as far back as you can, get a running start, and slam into it with your shoulder. At the same time, I'll give it a good hard tug."

"Whatever you say, mister!"

Habst let go of the partition, flipped around, and ran to the other end of the room. He spun and bolted at the partition with as much speed as he could gather, yelling "One, two, three!" as he ran. On "three," he slammed against the wall, shoulder first, putting the entire weight of his body into the blow.

At the same time, the man on the other side of the stage yanked at the base of the partition with what seemed to be superhuman force.

The motor underneath the turntable screeched, the chain attached to it jumped a sprocket, and the wall moved at least four more inches.

Monika's hand slumped to the ground. Habst pulled it from the crack.

"You both clear?" yelled the man.

"Yeah!" said Habst.

"Good! Now get as far back from the turntable as you can!"

Habst scooted away from the set, pulling Monika with him.

"Okay!" said Habst.

The man let go of the partition and it slammed backwards with a force that shook the whole building.

Habst pulled off his shirt and wrapped it tightly around Monika's wrist.

"Is the girl okay?" yelled the man from the other side of the stage.

"I don't know!" said Habst. "She's not conscious, but she's still breathing!"

"That's good, that's good! I'm sure somebody has called for help. I'm sorry, but I have to leave!"

The man jumped off the stage and ran out the door.

"Thank you, Walt Disney!" screamed Habst at the top of his lungs.

Habst looked down at Monika and softly patted her cheek.

"Stay with me," he said. "This was such a totally dumb idea. I never should have brought you with me."

"You didn't have a choice, asshole," said Monika, opening her eyes and smiling weakly.

Habst gasped.

"Most exciting day of my life," she said. "Wouldn't have missed it for the world."

He held her tightly until three paramedics raced in. They loaded her onto a stretcher and wheeled her to the parking lot behind the building, where she was put into an ambulance and rushed to the Celebration ER.

Charlie breathlessly ran into the room seconds later, and Habst tried to lift himself off the floor, intending to make a run for it. But he'd dislocated his shoulder when he'd slammed into the wall. So, his arm gave out completely, and he fell to the floor, hit his head, and passed out.

He woke up a minute later to the sound of Charlie smacking him in the face.

"Wake up, Habst!" yelled Charlie.

"Cut it out!" said Habst.

Charlie knelt down next to him.

"I need to pop your shoulder back into place," said Charlie.

"Where's Walt Disney?" asked Habst.

"Who?!"

"Walt Disney. He saved Monika."

"You're in a lot of pain. You don't know what you're saying."

"No... I swear... it was Walt...."

"Hold still. This is going to hurt."

Charlie grabbed Habst's forearm, pivoted it to a ninety-degree angle, and twisted it inward, popping his shoulder back into its socket.

Habst screamed and passed out again.

# Fourteen

THE URBAN LEGENDS surrounding Walt Disney's death range from the ridiculous (that he was cryogenically frozen) to the mundane (that his last words were "Kurt Russell"), but one thing they all have in common is that they're verifiably false.

Except for one.

As the story goes, soon after Walt died, a lawyer carrying a sealed reel of film rounded up the Company's ten highest ranking staff members, and brought them to a screening room.

Laid out on the theater's plush seats were name cards for each executive, artist, or engineer. The cards were evenly staggered across the chairs. When Donn Tatum lifted up his card and started to move down his aisle to sit next to Joe Fowler, the lawyer gently grabbed Tatum's arm and directed him back to his assigned seat.

The lawyer then instructed Roy O. Disney to crack the seal on the reel, thread it through the projector, and play the film. The lawyer left the room and posted a security guard in the hallway to make sure nobody got close enough to hear what was going on inside.

As the lights dimmed and the film began to play, the men were shocked to see their deceased boss on the screen, standing in his office and looking straight at them. Over the course of the thirty-minute reel, Walt proceeded to point directly at each of his former co-workers, address them by name, and tell them in detail what their duties would be over the next ten years, complete with exact deadlines for the completion of specific milestones.

When the film finished, nobody spoke. The men felt as if they'd just seen a ghost.

Finally, Roy Disney stood up, told everyone to remain seated, walked into the projection room, and quickly returned to the theater, film reel in hand.

An hour later, the entire group exited the theater, somberly marching in a single file line. A few of them had obviously been crying. Roger Broggie had a black eye.

That evening, the custodial staff found a pile of melted celluloid in one of the screening room's trash cans.

It was surmised that the men saw the film and realized that Walt's demands and goals were completely unrealistic. So, they decided to destroy the film, never mention it again, and proceed with running the Company the way they thought it should be run. And the rest is history: the quality of the Studio's releases declined rapidly, the construction of the Mineral King resort turned into a PR fiasco, and EPCOT was built as a theme park, not a city.

However, on his deathbed, one of the ten men told a family member this remarkable story, and insisted that Walt's directives had been followed to a tee, albeit entirely in secret. He claimed that the first of those directives had been telling Roy to destroy the film immediately after it had been viewed. And that the second of those directives had been to build Progress City. And that Progress City had indeed been built....

While the dying executive's claims were dismissed as a product of late-stage dementia, the story continues to circulate.

What is perhaps most telling is that none of the other men who were reported to be in that screening room ever went on the record regarding the circumstances of that day, despite decades of questioning from Disney historians and fans alike.

And so, although Snopes has marked this story as "Status: False", in the eyes of this author and many others, it is one of the few Disney urban legends that can legitimately be marked as "Status: Undetermined".

# Fifteen

Habst woke up in a jail cell. He rubbed his shoulder and slowly swung his arm around, wincing. It was still stiff, but his range of movement was normal.

He walked over to the bars of the cell.

"Hey!" he yelled. "Anybody there?"

A guard walked up to him.

"'Bout time you woke up, Princess."

"My girlfriend, Monika. Is she okay?"

"I don't know nuthin' 'bout her," said the guard. "All I know is Charlie told me to call him when you woke up."

The guard belched, ambled over to a phone, and dialed a number.

"Sleeping Beauty finally woke up. Yeah. Okay, I'll tell him."

The guard walked over to Habst.

"Your girlfriend is fine."

"Thank god!"

"They're holding you on a million-dollar bail."

"Holy shit!"

"You must have a fairy godmother, though. It's already been paid. You can leave."

"Seriously?"

"Charlie Walker wants you to stay put until he gets here."

"Do I have to?"

"No, you don't gotta. But you don't want to piss Charlie off."

"Eh, I have a long, long history of pissing Charlie off. I think I'll risk it."

"Whatever you say, Princess," said the guard, unlocking the cell door.

Habst checked out and collected his belongings. His fake ID had been seized. He opened the pocket of his backpack and saw that they'd also taken his pipe and bag of Blueberry Cheese.

"Jerks," said Habst.

He stepped out of the Kissimmee police station, saw Charlie's boring 2002 beige Camry pulling up, and bolted around the corner. He watched Charlie walk into the jail, and then ran in the opposite direction.

A few seconds later, he saw a cab, and hailed it. The cab stopped, and he jumped in.

"Where ya headin' pal?" asked the cabbie.

"Celebration Hospital," said Habst. He paused. "Can I pay you in virtcoins?"

The cabbie turned around and gave him a look of utter confusion.

"It's just that I don't have any cash," continued Habst. "But if you give me your wallet address, I can send you double whatever the cab ride costs. In virtcoins."

"My wallet address?" said the cabbie. "Buddy, my wallet don't got no address. It's in my pocket, and the only money I put in it is good old American dollars. I don't know what the hell dirtcoins are, but if you ain't got no dollars, you gotta get the hell out of my cab."

"VIRTcoins," said Habst. "V-I-R-T."

"Get outta here, asshole!" yelled the cabbie.

Habst threw his hands up and exited the cab, giving the driver the finger as he sped off.

Not knowing what else to do, he started walking in the direction of Celebration, which was a good ten miles away. He had to see Monika, make sure she was okay, and tell her about how Walt Disney had saved her.

After about a mile, he turned around and stuck his thumb up. Car after car passed him by. He looked down and noticed his clothes were caked in a mixture of Monika's blood and *Carousel of Progress* grease.

"Crap," said Habst.

He continued the futile attempt to hitch a ride, keeping his thumb up, but not bothering to walk backwards.

He heard a car slowing, and turned around.

"Dammit," he said, as he saw Charlie's Camry pull up next to him.

"Get in the car, Habst," said Charlie.

"No way."

"C'mon, Habst, don't be a stubborn fool. I've got nothing on you. You're legally out on bail. So just let me give you a ride to the hospital so you can see your girlfriend, okay?"

Habst threw his arms up in resignation, grimaced, rubbed his shoulder, and got into the car.

"Still hurt?" asked Charlie.

"Yeah. Yeah, it does, Charlie. You could've been a little more gentle, you know?"

Charlie laughed, and pulled back out onto the road.

"What, and miss my opportunity to legally inflict a massive amount of pain on you? Not a chance, Habst. Not a chance."

Habst looked at Charlie and grinned.

"Yeah, I guess I would've done the same for you."

"I know you would've, buddy," said Charlie, slapping him on the shoulder, hard. "I know you would've."

# Sixteen

IT WAS THE SMELL of death and peppermint that had first brought Habst to Charlie Walker's attention.

Everyone in the Company had heard of Charlie, of course. His single-handed takedown of a terrorist organization that had planned to kill a bunch of people on Space Mountain was legendary. But Habst hadn't met the guy in person. He tried to avoid anyone from Security whenever possible. So he wasn't exactly thrilled when his supervisor told him he'd been summoned to Charlie's office above Main Street.

"Why do I need to go, exactly?" asked Habst.

"Don't ask questions, just go," said his supervisor.

"Okay, but why?"

"That information is on a need-to-know basis, and you don't need to know."

"That's ridiculous. I mean, I'm going to find out when I get there, right?"

"Maybe you will, maybe you won't."

"You don't actually have any idea why he called me up there, do you?"

"Sure I do."

"Okay. So tell me, then."

"No."

"Yes."

"Shut the fuck up and get your ass to Security, Habst."

"You shut up."

"You're fired."

"Does that mean I don't have to go to Security?"

"No. Go to Security. Then you're fired."

"So if I don't go, I won't be fired?"

"No, you're fired either way."

"So what's the point in me going, then?"

"Goddammit, Habst! Get your ass to Security! I promise I won't fire you if you just go now!"

"Okay. I guess I'll go, then."

"Thank you. Christ."

So, Habst trudged slowly through the Utilidors to Main Street, took the stairway up to Building MO5, and knocked on Charlie's door.

"Come in," said a strong voice.

Habst opened the door and walked into a windowless, threadbare office. The walls were yellow-painted concrete blocks completely devoid of any art, photos, certificates, or awards. Charlie's desk was only slightly less bare. On it were an ancient HP Pavilion desktop, a phone, an air freshener shaped like a Mickey waffle, and a single framed photo that faced towards the famous detective.

"Close the door behind you," said Charlie.

Habst closed the door.

"Take a seat," said Charlie.

Habst sat.

"You're Reginald?"

"Habst."

Charlie looked over at his computer monitor, squinted, and turned back to Habst.

"Okay, Habst. Do you know why I've called you here?"

"No, but whatever it is, I didn't do it."

Charlie nodded, and looked back at his computer.

"Seems like you've received a lot of reprimands for being caught in backstage areas that you're not authorized to be in."

"That's not true."

"No point in lying, Habst. I might be new, but I'm not stupid. It's all right here in front of me," said Charlie, pointing to the screen. "You definitely have a long list of reprimands."

"Oh, yeah, that part is true. I just meant the part about not being authorized to be there. I'm a janitor. I'm pretty much authorized to be wherever there's dirt."

"That's an interesting leap of logic. Says here you were caught on the roof of Columbia Harbour House last week?"

"Yeah. The roof was dirty."

"It also says that the security officer who caught you claimed that the whole area reeked of marijuana."

"I had bad gas."

"Your gas smells like marijuana?"

"Apparently."

"Uh huh. Okay, look, enough of this nonsense."

"Yeah, I agree. Enough of this nonsense. Enough."

Charlie stared at Habst. Habst smiled. Charlie sighed.

"Look, the fart talk is actually surprisingly apropos here. Guest Services has recently received numerous complaints of a strange smell on Main Street. More specifically, the smell of a dead animal. At first it was just dismissed it as a rat that had died in a vent somewhere, but apparently it's getting worse."

"Oh yeah. I totally smelled that last night."

"You did? Well, good. Because I need you to help me track it down."

"Huh? What do you care? I don't see why this has anything to do with Security. And why me? Anyone in Custodial should be able to find a dead rat in a vent."

"No, I don't think so. I think it's going to be a little more difficult than that. I have a hunch about this smell, and I need someone who knows every nook and cranny of this place to help me track it down. When I contacted Custodial with that very request, your supervisor immediately recommended you."

"Wait, so now it's a good thing that I'm always sneaking around backstage?"

"I don't know if that's the right way to look at it, but…."

"Yeah, see, that's not cool, man. You can't be punishing me for something one second, and then telling me it's an asset to the Company the next. Make up your mind, already!"

"Fair enough. How about this? If you help me find where that smell is coming from, I'll wipe those reprimands off your record. Not only that, but I'll tell my staff that as long as you're employed with the Company, they are not to detain you if you're found backstage."

"Even if I'm found somewhere that smells like marijuana farts?"

"Even if you're found somewhere that smells like marijuana farts."

"You've got yourself a deal."

Habst stood up and shook Charlie's hand.

"Great," said Charlie. "Now let's find out where that smell is coming from. Meet me at the Hub at midnight."

"You got it, Boss!" said Habst.

---

THAT NIGHT, HABST met Charlie at the Hub, the Magic Kingdom's central plaza.

"Thanks for coming," said Charlie.

"Wouldn't miss it for anything," said Habst.

"Most of the reports say that the smell is strongest at the beginning of Main Street, near the Railroad station."

"Yeah, that's where I smelled it."

"Okay, good. So let's just start walking down Main Street, and maybe between the two of us, we can determine a point of origin. You take the West side, and I'll take the East side."

"Got it."

Habst crossed over to the right, Charlie crossed to the left, and they both walked slowly down Main Street, noses in the air.

"I smell cookies," said Charlie.

"That's the Main Street Bakery," said Habst. "They pipe in the smell through vents at the bottom of the shop using a contraption called a Smellitzer. Supposed to draw people into the bakery to buy shit."

"Interesting…," said Charlie.

They continued on, past the alley that dead-ended at Charlie's office, past the defunct Main Street Cinema, and past the main entrance to the Emporium. As they neared the end of the street, Charlie held up a finger.

"There. Smell that?"

Habst crossed the street to where Charlie was standing. He sniffed.

"Yeah."

"Smells like a dead animal… and… peppermint?"

Habst turned, and looked up.

"The Main Street Confectionery. Of course."

"Of course, what?" asked Charlie.

"Another Smellitzer. It pumps out a peppermint scent all day."

Habst ran over to the edge of the building and got on his hands and knees.

"What are you doing?" asked Charlie.

"Looking for the vent," said Habst.

He crawled a few more feet, stopped, and pointed to a six-inch round metal-screened hole, painted the same color as the trim around it.

"There it is."

Habst put his nose up to it, sniffed, and recoiled.

"Oh, man, that's awful!"

Charlie bent down, sniffed, and also recoiled.

"Death and peppermint," he said. "Not a pleasant

combination. Okay, so where's the Smellitzer that's pushing this scent out?"

"Downstairs."

"Lead the way."

Habst led Charlie backstage, and into the Utilidors.

"It smells terrible down here," said Charlie.

"Yeah, that's the way it always smells," said Habst. "Like rotting garbage."

They walked to the location directly under the Main Street Confectionery.

"Uh, let's see," said Habst. "If I remember correctly, the Smellitzer is in an unmarked door right over… oh, yeah, here it is."

Habst yanked at the door. It wouldn't budge.

"It's locked," said Habst.

"Dammit," said Charlie.

"It's okay, I've got a full set of master keys right here."

He pulled out a large ring of at least two-dozen keys.

"What the hell, Habst?!" said Charlie. "You shouldn't have those!"

"Why not? Locks don't stop dirt, man. I got a job to do, right?"

"No. No. No no no no no. No! Dammit, you should not have those!"

"But I bet you're glad I do right about now, though, huh?" asked Habst, picking a key from the chain, inserting it into the door, and turning.

The lock clicked. Habst turned the handle, and pulled open the door.

The stench knocked them both to the ground. Habst vomited.

Charlie stood, held his arm over his nose, and walked into the small room, which was barely bigger than a closet. Inside was a machine with a fan, which was hooked to a large steel drum on the floor. The label on the drum read:

FLAVORSCENTS

Division of

FLAVOR & FRAGANCE SPECIALTIES
8800-P KELSO DRIVE
BALTIMORE, MARYLAND 21221

WALT DISNEY WORLD CO.
1475 N. AVE. OF THE STARS / TRAILER W294
LAKE BUENA VISTA, FL 32830

PEPPERMINT SCENT FRAGRANCE 71379
PO# GACGO1579

LOT # 60530
NET 55 GALLONS

Habst walked in, his shirt wrapped around his nose and mouth, and pointed to the drum.

"It's in the barrel, Charlie. Whatever is causing the smell is in there with the peppermint scent!"

Charlie nodded and walked over to the drum.

"Give me your key ring," he said to Habst.

Habst threw him the keys. Charlie took one, and used it to pry open the lid of the drum. The lid fell to the floor with a loud clang, and Habst jumped.

Charlie slowly leaned forward and peered into the drum.

"Jesus," he said, jolting back.

"What's in there, Charlie?" asked Habst, inching towards the drum.

"Get out of here, Habst!" said Charlie, waving him away. "You don't need to see this."

"Why, what is it?"

"I'm going to need a list of every Smellitzer in Walt Disney World."

"Dammit, Charlie, what's in the drum?!"

Charlie shook his head and slumped against the wall.

"We've found one of our missing Cast Members."

---

After that evening, Habst didn't see much of Charlie. Not for a while, anyway. But in the following weeks, he heard through the grapevine that two more Cast Members had been found in Smellitzer drums: one in the burning Rome barrel in Epcot's Spaceship Earth, and one in the stinkbug barrel in Animal Kingdom's *It's Tough to Be a Bug*.

From what little info Habst was able to gather, it was only after Charlie posted Security 24/7 at every Smellitzer site throughout the resort that a face character was apprehended dragging a dead body into the room that housed the orange scent in Soarin'.

But as hard as Habst tried, he couldn't find any further details about the case. Nobody knew for sure who the dead Cast Members were. Rumors swirled around the break rooms, but there was so much turnover in the Company that it was impossible to attribute any unexplained absences to anything malicious. And certainly none of the low-level grunts that Habst hung out with had any leads on who the murderer was, much less what their motive might have been.

Charlie eventually refused to even acknowledge the existence of the dead body they'd found together. He told Habst it was a raccoon, and that Habst must have heard him wrong.

In the end, the entire thing was covered up so tightly that nobody even seemed to remember it had happened....

But hell, Charlie had kept his end of the bargain, and had given Habst free reign of Walt Disney World. As long as he was a Cast Member, he could go backstage, smoke up wherever he wanted, and not get hassled by Security. So even though some of the stuff Charlie was investigating seemed ultra-shady, and the way he went about his job was a little too Black Ops for Habst's tastes, the dude was pretty okay in his book.

# SEVENTEEN

CHARLIE AND HABST ENTERED the intensive care wing at Celebration Hospital, and went up to the desk in the waiting room.

"Monika Purcelli?" asked Habst.

"Room twenty-four," said the receptionist, handing him two visitor stickers.

"You go ahead," said Charlie. "I'll wait out here."

"Okay, cool."

"And Habst, don't even think about making a run for it."

Habst smiled and went down the hallway to room twenty-four.

He opened the door and saw Ms. Purcelli standing over a crying Monika, stroking her hair. Monika's hand was heavily bandaged and splinted. Ms. Purcelli looked up, saw Habst, and started yelling.

"You son of a bitch! You bastard! You cocksucker! You did this to my daughter! You've ruined her life! She can't do any more modeling shoots! How are we going to pay our bills? We're going to lose the house because of you, you filthy bum cocksucker! Get out of here! Get out of our house! Get out of our lives!"

Ms. Purcelli ran at him and swung her abnormally large

purse at his bad shoulder. Habst howled in pain and fell to the ground. She started beating him over the head with the purse. He covered his head and collapsed into a fetal position.

"Ow! What the hell, Ms. Purcelli?!"

Charlie ran in, quickly assessed the scene, and jumped in front of Ms. Purcelli.

"Calm down, ma'am," said Charlie. "You keep hitting this boy and you'll be arrested for assault."

Habst stood up and limped over to Monika's bed.

"Oh, Habst, how could you?" said Monika, sobbing.

"How could I what?" asked Habst. "I mean, I'm really sorry about the electric bills. I'll figure out some way to pay your mom back. But you said today was the most exciting day of your life and you wouldn't have missed it for anything, right?"

"You idiot!" yelled Ms. Purcelli. "Putting my daughter's life at risk! You horrible, terrible man! I want you gone!"

"Not the goddamned bills, Habst!" said Monika. "You've been fucking my mother, you asshole! How could you?!"

"Oh, shit," said Habst.

Charlie turned away from Ms. Purcelli and stared at Habst, mouth agape.

"You slept with your girlfriend's mother?"

"So… I mean… it's just that… I swear I didn't enjoy a second of it!" said Habst, turning to Monika. "I swear! It was awful!"

"You son of a bitch!" screamed Ms. Purcelli, knocking Charlie out of the way and running full-force at Habst.

He quickly sidestepped, held out his arm, and clotheslined her. Ms. Purcelli caught air and landed flat on her back. Her head smacked onto the floor, knocking her cold.

"That was totally self-defense, Charlie!" said Habst. "You saw the whole thing! If she's dead, that was totally self-defense, dammit!"

Monika started freaking out.

"You killed my mom?!" she screamed. "First you fuck her,

then you kill her?! You sick, twisted, son of a bitch! Get out of here, Habst, get out! I never want to see you again!"

Charlie kneeled down and checked Ms. Purcelli's pulse.

"She's not dead."

"Bummer," said Habst.

"Get out!" yelled Monika.

"Monika, look, it's just that she kept threatening to evict me from the house, and I didn't want to leave you, and… and… I had no choice, dammit!"

Monika sobbed uncontrollably.

"Just get out of here, Habst. Just leave. Please, leave."

He went over to her bed and tried to kiss her.

"Get out, you fucking asshole!" she screamed, thrashing around in the bed like a crazy person.

"C'mon, Habst," said Charlie, pulling him away from the bed.

"Monika, I swear, I just wanted to keep living there with you! I promise, that's the only reason I did it!"

Monika kept crying as Charlie pushed Habst out of the room.

---

"Damn, you sure have a way of getting yourself into some bad situations," said Charlie as he walked Habst to the car.

"Story of my life, Charlie. Story of my life."

They got into the car, and Habst leaned his head back onto the padded headrest.

"Charlie?"

"Yeah?"

"What'd you do with my pipe and my Blueberry Cheese?"

"They're in the evidence room at the Kissimmee police station."

"That sucks."

"Protocol."

"Protocol sucks."

Charlie shook his head, cranked the engine, and drove out of the hospital garage.

"Where to?" asked Charlie.

"Guess I better get my crap outta Monika's place."

"And then?"

"Beats me, man."

Charlie looked at him and sighed.

"Against my better judgment, you can hole up at my place until you get back on your feet."

Habst spun around.

"Really, Charlie? Really?! You'd do that for me?"

"Sure, Habst. It's not a big deal. We have a guest room. But you have to promise, promise on your life – because I will kill you if you break this promise – you have to promise not to lay a hand on my daughters or my wife."

"I promise," said Habst. "Wait. How old are your daughters?"

"Seriously?" Charlie looked at Habst in disbelief. Habst stared back at him. "Christ, you're serious. Violet is nine, and Katie is seven."

"Yeah, that's way too young for me. How old is your wife?"

"Habst!"

"What?!"

"She's thirty-two, dammit!"

"Yeah. Way too old for me. Shouldn't be a problem, Charlie. I can confidently promise that I won't touch your daughters or your wife."

"You have major issues, you know that?"

Habst shrugged.

---

WHEN THEY PULLED into Monika's driveway, Habst started freaking out.

"My stuff! All of my stuff! They dumped it all outside!

What the hell, man?!"

Habst bent over his server rack, which was lying sideways on the concrete. Pieces of plastic and metal were strewn everywhere.

"My mining rig!" yelled Habst. "They destroyed my mining rig!"

He picked up a cracked spindle from a hard drive and threw it across the yard.

"You can sue them for that," said Charlie, stepping out of the car. "There's a pretty strict due process when it comes to evicting tenants."

"To hell with due process, Charlie! They broke my mining servers!" Habst collapsed to the ground next to his rack. "All that money, down the drain. Think about all the weed I could've bought with that money, Charlie! Think of the weed!"

"Yeah, you really shouldn't be telling me that."

Habst stood up, defeated.

"Can you help me load this stuff into the car?"

"Sure. But where are the rest of your belongings? Furniture, books, papers, clothes?"

"There," said Habst, pointing to a steamer trunk. "My clothes are all in there. And it has a false bottom, which is where I keep important stuff."

He walked over to the trunk, opened it, dug down past the clothes, lifted up the false bottom, pulled out a *Playboy*, shook it out, and pointed at the centerfold.

"Sara Jean Underwood. Playmate of the Year, 2007. Hottest girl I've ever seen in my life. Aside from Monika, of course."

"That's your important stuff? *Playboy*s?"

"Uh… yeah?" said Habst, looking at Charlie like he was crazy.

"One man's trash…," said Charlie.

Ignoring him, Habst pulled a book out of the bottom of the trunk.

"*Fear and Loathing in Las Vegas*. Signed. He made the

inscription out to me! Look!"

Habst opened the book.

*To Habst, one of the most annoying motherfuckers I've ever had the displeasure to meet – Hunter S. Thompson.*

"Isn't that awesome?!"

"…is another man's treasure," continued Charlie.

"Whatever, man. You got no taste. You're all domesticated and stuff. Now can you stop judging me and help me load all of this into the car?"

"Sure," said Charlie.

"Okay, great," said Habst. "You do that, and I'll be right back."

Habst ran towards the shed behind the house, leaving Charlie to load the car himself.

"Habst?" yelled Charlie.

"I'll be right back!" yelled Habst over his shoulder.

"Lazy bum," said Charlie, as he hoisted the steamer trunk into the Camry.

Habst ran into the shed, pulled a strip of carpet from the floor, lifted the trapdoor underneath, and climbed down into the tunnel. Crouching, he walked all the way through the tunnel to the basement of the house, until he reached the location of his safe. He pulled out the rock, removed his safe, replaced the rock, blew a kiss at the back of his life-sized poster of Sara Jean Underwood, and ran back through the tunnel and up into the shed.

Charlie was pushing the server rack into the backseat of the car.

"Give me a hand with this, dammit!" yelled Charlie.

Habst ran up to the car, opened the opposite back door, got in, and lifted up the end of the server rack.

"Okay, now push!" said Habst.

Charlie pushed, and the rack slid into the car.

"Phew!" said Habst. "That was a lot of work."

Charlie, doubled over and breathless, lifted his head, looked at Habst, raised his arm, and gave him the middle finger.

"Where did you run off to?" asked Charlie, lowering his arm and breathing heavily.

"Had to get my safe," said Habst, shoving the safe into Charlie's face.

Charlie knocked it out of the way.

"What's in there? Cash?"

"Nope. I don't carry cash. I don't even own a wallet."

"Then how do you pay for food?"

Habst pointed at the mansion and smiled.

"You're right. Never mind. Stupid question. So what's in there, then? Social Security card?"

"Nope. Don't have one."

"You don't have one?! Birth certificate? Passport? Driver's license?"

"Nope, nope, and nope. Lost it, can't afford to travel, and never learned to drive."

"You're a real piece of work, you know that?"

"That's what they tell me."

"So?"

"So...."

"So what's in the safe, Habst?!" yelled Charlie.

"Oh, right. Uh... naked pictures of Monika?"

"Uh huh."

"Naked pictures of your mom?"

"You know what? I don't care. Let's just get out of here. I'm tired and hungry, and I want to go back home and see my family."

"Kick ass," said Habst. "I haven't eaten for, like... uh... hmmm. I think the last time I ate was when Fatty gave me a bag of Combos while I was waiting for you to ban me!"

Charlie shook his head, and they got in the car and drove off.

# Eighteen

THE CAMRY PULLED into the driveway of the Walker household. The house was a fairly standard Florida rancher. It wasn't anything fancy, but it was in a nice subdivision. Charlie had obviously done well for himself over the years, but he didn't really seem like the sort of guy who was into extravagance or elegant living.

"Guess this is sort of slumming it for you, huh?" said Charlie.

"Nah. This is real nice, man," said Habst. "No joke. This is cool."

Charlie put his arm around Habst, and brought him through the front door.

"I'm home!" shouted Charlie. "And I have a guest, so nobody come out in your underwear!"

Habst looked at Charlie.

"When it's hot out Meghan doesn't like to wear a lot of clothes," said Charlie.

"Awww...."

"Stop. Now."

"...yeahhhh?"

"No. No 'aw yeah'. You promised, remember?"

A large German shepherd walked up to Habst and sniffed

his leg. The dog whined, shook his head, raised his eyebrows, and looked up at Charlie.

"It's okay, Zeus," said Charlie, patting the dog's head. "He might smell like a dumpster, but he's all right."

"Hey, Zeus!" said Habst. He scratched behind the dog's ears, and Zeus wagged his tail happily. "Man, I love dogs. Haven't had one since I was a kid. Couldn't afford the extra security deposit in the apartments I stayed in, and Ms. Purcelli hates animals."

Violet and Katie entered the room, immediately suspicious of the scruffy, bloody, dirty man standing in their foyer.

"Hi," said Habst, waving at them.

"Girls," said Charlie, "this is Habst. I've told you about him, remember?"

"Oh!" said Katie. "He's the dumb stoner troublemaker!"

"No, Katie," said Violet. "He's the dumb stoner troublemaker… with a heart of gold!"

"Oh, right," said Katie. "A heart of gold…."

"A heart of gold that's covered in filth," said Meghan, walking into the room with a robe on.

"Good," said Charlie. "You're not naked."

"She doesn't look thirty-two," whispered Habst to Charlie.

Charlie glared at him. Habst put on his best normal-person smile, and turned to the family.

"Hi, Katie. Hi, Violet. Hi, Mrs. Walker," said Habst, shaking everyone's hand.

"Hi, Habst!" shouted the girls.

Charlie squatted down until he was at eye-level with the girls.

"Habst is going to stay with us for a few days, if that's okay with you two," he said, and looked up at Meghan. "And with Mommy."

"Is he a criminal, Daddy?" asked Katie.

Charlie stood up and cleared his throat. Habst shuffled his feet.

"Well, technically, yes, he is," said Charlie.

Meghan walked over to her daughter and put her hand on her shoulder.

"I'm sure he's been unjustly accused, and that he presents no danger to anyone in this house. Right, Habst?" said Meghan.

"You can trust me, Mrs. Walker. I had a sister their age, and we were best friends."

"You have a sister?" said Charlie.

"Plus," continued Habst, ignoring him, "I'd never hurt a fly. Well, I mean, I did clothesline Ms. Purcelli earlier today, but she sorta brought that upon herself."

Meghan looked over at Charlie with a what-the-fuck look. Charlie laughed.

"Oh boy do we have some great stories to tell you tonight!"

"Yay!" shouted Violet and Katie. "Disney criminal stories!"

"So what do you think, girls? Can Habst stay here?"

Violet looked down at Katie, who nodded her approval.

"Sure," said Violet.

"Meghan?" said Charlie, looking at his wife.

"Sure," she said. "He needs a serious deep cleaning before he gets anywhere near our linens, though."

"Thanks a bunch, Mrs. Walker," said Habst. "Just point me to the shower and I'll get scrubbed down before I track any more muck into your nice house."

Meghan laughed.

"The bathroom is over there," she said, pointing. "Towels are under the sink. And please, stop with the Mrs. Walker stuff. We're almost the same age. Call me Meghan."

Habst nodded at her, and walked off to the bathroom.

"Girls," said Charlie. "Can you pick out a nice clean outfit for Habst from his steamer trunk over there, and then go put it in front of the bathroom door?"

"Sure, Daddy," said Violet and Katie. They ran off to the trunk, opened it, and started sifting through the clothes.

"It smells like smoke and flowers in here!" yelled Violet.

Zeus came up beside them, sniffed the inside of the trunk, and barked.

"Yes, sweetie. Smoke and flowers. Oh, and only pull from the top!" yelled Charlie. "Don't worry about the bottom layers."

He turned to Meghan.

"You don't even want to know what he's got under the false bottom of that thing," said Charlie.

She chuckled.

"Charlie Walker. Always picking up strays. You just can't help yourself, can you?"

"You're not going to believe what happened today."

"Crazier than last night?"

"Well, I mean, nobody got their hand stuck in an attraction, but yeah, it was still pretty wild. Habst seems to attract crazy situations like shit attracts flies."

"Gross, Charlie!"

"I think having him around is going to be good for this family, though," said Charlie. "We need some alternative culture around here. I don't want the girls heading into high school being all naïve about everything."

"Charlie, they were kidnapped by a master criminal and watched their father kick said master criminal out of Bay Lake Tower to his death. I'd hardly call them naïve."

"Well, yeah, there's that. But I just mean about normal stuff. Drugs and sex, you know?"

"I know what you mean, babe," said Meghan. "And I think it's sweet that you're trying to justify having him here. But it's not necessary. I'm as much of a sucker for strays as you are."

"Yeah…," said Charlie. "We're a couple of softies, huh?"

"We sure are, and I wouldn't have it any other way."

They hugged, and Charlie kissed her on the forehead.

"So," said Charlie, pulling away. "Habst says the last thing he had to eat was a bag of Combos two days ago."

Meghan laughed.

"I'm not entirely sure he was joking," said Charlie. "You

think you could cook something up for dinner?"

"Something better than a bag of Combos? Yeah, I think I can manage that."

She went into the kitchen, and Charlie walked around the corner to see what the girls were up to.

He found them peering around the bathroom door, which they'd opened just enough to see through it undetected by Habst.

"Girls!" yelled Charlie.

"Aw, man," said Katie. "Busted."

"He's cute, Daddy," said Violet. "And he has nicer leg muscles than you. And a bigger wee-wee."

"Are you kidding me?!" yelled Charlie. "Scram! Get out of here and go help your mother with dinner!"

"Something wrong, Charlie?" yelled Habst from the bathroom.

"No!" said Charlie, shooing the girls away. "Your clothes are right outside the door. We'll be getting dinner ready."

Charlie turned towards the kitchen.

"This should be an interesting night," he muttered to himself.

# NINETEEN

THAT EVENING, AT AROUND 6PM, there were fifteen people in the audience for *Walt Disney's Carousel of Progress*. Following the events of the evening before, Custodial had given the 1920s set a good scrub down to get rid of the bloodstains. But other than that, the ride operated as usual when the park opened that morning.

All was normal up to about halfway through the Christmas scene. John was cooking a turkey with a voice-activated oven and seriously messing it up. Jimmy and Grandma were playing a virtual reality game and Jimmy was getting his ass beat like the little bitch he was. Grandpa talked about laserdiscs, which made him sound like he had dementia. Patty just sat there doing nothing of worth, Rover looked like he was going to die, and Sarah was berating everyone.

Towards the end of the scene, Grandma yelled her final score and John repeated it, setting the voice-activated oven to an extremely high temperature, to the complete ignorance of everyone onstage. This part of the show was insulting to the audience, and was also insulting to the formerly intelligent characters that Walt Disney himself had created. The audience instinctively knew this, and they groaned at every lame joke made at the family's expense.

But then, as the oven timer counted down, something completely unexpected happened. Normally when the timer went off, the oven door blasted open and smoke came pouring out. This time, the oven door blew clear off its hinges with extreme force, flew across the room, decapitated John, kept going, decapitated Jimmy, continued downward, decapitated Grandma, and fell to the floor.

Oily hydraulic fluid spouted from their necks. John sagged forward, spurting fluid all over Rover. Jimmy's arms flailed around spastically. The game control dislodged from his hand, flew across the stage, and hit Grandpa in the face. Grandma's arm shot straight out and smashed a hole into the flat screen TV.

Someone in the audience screamed. Someone else cheered. Everyone else was too busy holding their phones up, filming the beautiful destruction of that final, horribly out-of-date, long-neglected scene.

*There's a Great Big Beautiful Tomorrow* started playing, and the theater rotated until the scene was out of sight.

The audience clapped and hooted and hollered, and ran out of the theater smiling and laughing, much to the confusion of the attraction's Cast Members, who were used to seeing Guests leave the theater looking bored and half-asleep.

# TWENTY

HABST ATE THREE-QUARTERS of a family-sized frozen lasagna all by himself. The kids stared at him in total disbelief as he shoveled food into his mouth faster than anyone they'd ever seen.

He picked up his empty plate, held it up to his face, licked it clean, put it down, pushed himself away from the table, and patted his stomach.

"So... I guess you were hungry, then?" asked Meghan.

"I sure was," he said. "Thanks for the grub. I might actually be able to take a dump tonight!"

Violet and Katie giggled.

"Okay, kids" said Charlie. "I think that's your cue to go into the other room and read some *Sherlock Holmes* or play a game of Clue or something."

"Time for adult talk," said Katie to Violet.

"He's barely more of an adult than we are," whispered Violet.

"Hey, I heard that!" said Habst.

"Into the other room girls! Scoot!" said Charlie.

The girls ran off, and Charlie turned to Habst.

"Okay, time for some serious talk."

"Oh man, c'mon," said Habst.

"First things, first. Who bailed you out? I'd assumed it was Ms. Purcelli, but that obviously wasn't the case. A million dollars is a lot of money to be on the hook for."

"Uh… a rich uncle?"

"A rich uncle. Right."

"Sure. My Uncle Walt. Cool dude."

"Okay, fine. Don't tell me," said Charlie, pulling a piece of paper out of his pocket. "Next order of business: a list of what you were charged with last night."

He unfolded the paper and set it on the table in front of Habst.

"Oh wow," said Meghan, looking at it. "That is a very, very long list."

"Yes, it is," said Charlie. "Habst, I need you to understand the seriousness of these charges."

"Hold on a second, Charlie," said Habst, standing up. "I'll be right back."

Habst ran into the other room. Charlie looked at Meghan and shrugged. A few seconds later Habst ran back into the room with his safe. He put the safe on the table, opened it, and pulled out a bag of weed and his vaporizer.

"Tell me that is not what I think it is," said Charlie. "You honestly cannot be this dumb."

"Whatever, dude. There's no way I'm listening to this crap unless I'm blitzed. Plus, you're even not a real cop anymore. So loosen up!" He turned to Meghan. "There's no smell from the vaporizer, but I can take this outside if you want. Your house, your rules."

"Really? No smell?" asked Meghan.

"Nope. Well, I mean, no smoke or pot odor. The vapor kinda smells like popcorn."

"Well, as long as the kids can't smell it, I'm fine with you smoking…"

"Vaping," said Habst.

"…vaping in here," finished Meghan.

"Cool, thanks!"

"I am not supporting this," said Charlie.

Habst ignored him, loaded up the chamber of the WISPR, flicked the igniter, waited a few seconds for it to get to the right temperature, and then took a big long toke.

Charlie shook his head and pointed to the sheet of paper.

"First charge: possession of less than twenty grams of marijuana. Misdemeanor with maximum incarceration of one year, maximum one thousand dollar fine. Second charge: possession of paraphernalia. Misdemeanor. Same jail term, same fine."

"That's some real bullshit right there," said Habst, taking another hit.

"Look," said Charlie. "It doesn't matter what you think about the law. The judge won't care if you don't agree with it. The fact is, you were caught with a bag of pot and a pipe, and now you're looking at two misdemeanors, jail time, and a big fine. And that's not even the start of it!"

He pointed at the sheet again.

"Third charge: trespassing. Since you were already warned, it's a first-degree misdemeanor. Up to a year in jail and a thousand dollar fine. It's adding up, isn't it Habst?"

"Whatever, man."

"Not 'whatever'. This is serious business. And we haven't even gotten to the real bad stuff yet. For example, charge number four: contributing to the delinquency of a minor. First-degree misdemeanor. One year, one thousand dollars."

"Oh, come on!" said Habst.

"Yeah, Ms. Purcelli wants to throw the book at you. And if Monika wants to, she can get you for statutory rape. And that, my friend, is a felony with a ten thousand dollar fine and fifteen years in the state pen."

"That's insane! She's my girlfriend. I didn't rape her! Hell, if anything, there were times were I'd say she raped me." He turned to Meghan. "That girl always wants the dick."

Meghan blushed.

"But that's hypothetical right now," continued Charlie. "Let's stick with actual charges. Burglary. Felony, ten thousand dollars and fifteen years."

"What the hell?!" yelled Habst. "Burglary?! What did I burgle?"

"The definition of burglary is 'entry into a building illegally with intent to commit a crime' and I think what you did fits that charge perfectly well."

"You're screwed," said Meghan.

"Exactly," said Charlie.

Habst put his head in his hands.

"I'm screwed."

"And, I'm saving my favorite for last: forgery! You were carrying a fake Cast Member ID. And for that you get a felony charge, a five thousand dollar fine, and five years in prison. What the hell were you doing with a fake ID, Habst?"

"I used to use it to get on the Cast Member bus so I wouldn't have to pay for a park ticket. And then if I was going backstage I'd wear it so nobody would hassle me."

"How do you even get a fake Disney ID?"

"Off of Galt's Gulch. Same place I got this," he said, holding up the bag of weed. "Dude did a great job. I sent him a bunch of pictures of current IDs, gave him exact measurements, everything. I even went to BDubs on Cast Member night and used a portable RFID reader to copy the info from this drunk College Program chick's ID. Then my dude hacked that code, made up a new identity for me, and wrote it onto the fake's RFID chip. That damn ID could open every door in the entire resort. Sucks that it's locked up in the Kissimmee evidence room now."

"It's not," said Charlie. "I asked for it back so I could examine it and decide if we were going forward with those forgery charges."

"Goddammit," said Habst. "I shouldn't have told you all of

that, then. That's entrapment or something!"

"I'm not the one who ordered a forged ID from the Darknet, Habst! You're the criminal here, not me!"

"Screw you, Charlie! I never did anything bad with it. I never damaged any property, and I never stole anything. I never did anything except for exploring and videotaping. So stick your goddamned forgery charge up your ass and sit on it."

Charlie stood, crumpled the rap sheet into a ball, and threw it at Habst.

"There's no getting through to you, is there? Your girlfriend is in the hospital, you've made me look completely inept, and you're facing a huge fine and years in jail. Yet you're still insisting you've done nothing wrong?! Pull your head out of the ground and look around, Habst. You're in serious trouble here, and you need to man up and deal with it like a responsible adult for once in your wasted, insignificant life."

"I don't need this kinda crap," said Habst, standing up. "I'm outta here."

"Good riddance," said Charlie.

"Habst, no!" yelled Meghan, as Habst grabbed his safe and walked out of the kitchen. "Charlie, you better not let him leave this house. If he leaves, you're sleeping on the couch for at least a month."

Charlie's cell phone rang.

"I have to take this," he said.

She stared at him, hands on hips.

"Fine. Go get him," said Charlie. "I'll be there as soon as I get off this call, and we'll sort things out."

"Thank you," she said, kissing him before running out of the kitchen.

"Charlie Walker here," he said, turning his attention to the phone.

"Charlie, it's Bill Ivers, CEO of the Disney Company. How are you tonight?

"Uh, I'm fine, sir. It's an honor to speak with you. Quite unusual for you to be calling me, though. I think the last time you called was after the Holloway incident."

"Well, these are unusual circumstances. Do you have time to chat? I didn't catch you in the middle of anything, did I?"

"No, no, now is a fine time to talk. What's on your mind, sir?

"Well, Charlie, it looks like we had an act of sabotage in the Magic Kingdom this evening. The final scene of the *Carousel of Progress* has pretty much been destroyed."

"Oh my god! Was anyone hurt?

"No, no injuries, thankfully. We actually received some positive comments at City Hall about it, to be honest."

"Uh…."

"Look, Charlie, we've got a real problem on our hands here. We think this Reginald Habstermeister fellow is deliberately sabotaging rides."

"No disrespect, sir, but that's impossible."

"Oh? How so?"

"Because he's been with me since he left the station this afternoon. Hasn't left my sight all day."

"Well, that's a pretty solid alibi."

"I'd say so."

"Regardless, we need to get to the bottom of this, and fast. There's only so much longer we can keep the press in the dark, not to mention the FBI and the NSA. And god forbid OSHA catches wind of it. I want this handled internally and kept quiet. Think you and this Reginald fellow can meet me in an hour to hash out a plan to deal with this fiasco?"

Charlie looked around the corner, and saw Habst standing next to the front door, safe in hand. Meghan said something to him, and he put the safe down and hugged her. Zeus, who was standing next to them, lifted his paw and offered it to Habst. Habst smiled, shook it, wiped a tear from his eye, and walked down the hallway towards the guest room.

"Sure, I think that'll work," said Charlie. "Where would you like to meet, sir?"

"I'll clear out Mizner's at the Grand Floridian. See you and the boy there in an hour."

"10-4, Mr. Ivers," said Charlie, disconnecting the call.

He walked into the living room and yelled down the hallway.

"Habst?! You up for a drink with the CEO of the Disney Company?"

"Sure!" said Habst, poking his head out of the bedroom. "Will the Pope and Barack Obama be there, too?"

"The way this day is going, it's entirely possible," said Charlie.

# TWENTY-ONE

CHARLIE AND HABST WALKED into the lobby of the Grand Floridian, took the elevator to the second floor, turned left, and headed to Mizner's.

Two huge men in suits stood at either side of the entrance. The one on the left held out his arm.

"The bar is closed. Have a magical day."

"Outta the way, goon," said Habst, and continued walking.

Faster than Habst could blink, the thug slammed him onto the floor and put him in a sleeper hold.

"Ughghg," gurgled Habst.

"We're here to see Mr. Ivers," said Charlie.

"Stand down, boys," said Ivers, walking out of the bar.

The thug let Habst go. Habst got to his knees, gasping for breath, looked up, and saw Bill Ivers standing over him, smiling.

Ivers was dressed in a dark sport coat, a crisp blue-and-white checkered shirt with the top button undone, khakis, and dock shoes. His hair was immaculately coiffed, and his skin was so smooth and perfectly tanned that he looked like he was wearing makeup.

Habst hated him immediately.

"Good to see you again, old friend," said Ivers, shaking

Charlie's hand. "Seems like we only meet up when something bad is happening. I'll have to fly you out to Pebble Beach for golf and a steak once this mess blows over."

"Nice to see you, too, Mr. Ivers," said Charlie. "And I'd love to take you up on that offer."

"Good, good," said Ivers. He turned to Habst, who had finally caught his breath and stood up. "And I assume this is the infamous rabble-rouser Reginald Habstermeister?"

"Yeah," said Habst, shaking Ivers' hand. "You can call me Habst."

"You've got a very unique name, son," said Ivers.

"The last name is German," said Habst. "And the first name…. Well, that came from my dad. He was a real dick. You kinda remind me of him, actually."

Ivers stared at Habst for a second, blinked, smiled politely, and turned to Charlie.

"Alright, then," he said. "Now that the pleasantries are out of the way, why don't you two join me for a drink and we'll get down to brass tacks."

They walked into the dark bar, which overlooked the back of the Grand Floridian and the Seven Seas Lagoon.

"What's your poison?" asked Ivers.

"Scotch, neat." said Charlie.

"Good man," said Ivers. "And you, Reginald?"

"Hell, I don't know. I don't really drink. I'm more of a smoking man, if you get my drift."

"I did notice those charges on your rap sheet from last night," said Ivers. "But this is a drinking establishment, son, so what'll it be?"

Habst didn't like being talked down to and called 'son'. He felt like punching Bill Ivers in his smug tanned face.

"Whatever, man," said Habst.

"Three Lagavulin 16s, neat," yelled Ivers to the bartender, and then motioned to a table. "Let's sit over by this window here. Lovely view. I don't get over to the Florida property as often as I'd like. But whenever I do, I make it a point to get a drink here at Mizner's. It's a bit of a tradition for me."

"Happy to share in that tradition, sir," said Charlie, taking a seat.

"Do you always clear out the bar like a rich douchebag so paying guests can't enjoy it?" asked Habst.

"Habst!" yelled Charlie.

"Haha, no, it's perfectly alright," said Ivers. "I'm always interested in hearing the opinions of the unwashed masses."

Habst glared at him.

"That was a joke, son," said Ivers.

"Uh huh," said Habst.

The bartender came to the table and set down three scotches.

"Here's to clearing up this mess at the parks," said Ivers. "Cheers."

They all sipped their drinks. The scotch burned Habst's throat, and he started coughing.

"Take it like a man," said Ivers, smacking him on the back.

"Don't touch me," said Habst, continuing to cough.

Ivers put his drink down, and looked Habst straight in the eyes.

"You're in real trouble, Reginald, and I'm here to help you out of that trouble. If you want to keep from being ass raped for the rest of your life in a federal penitentiary, I suggest you show a little more respect."

Habst seethed, and said nothing. He looked at Charlie, who nodded back understandingly. Charlie turned to Ivers.

"What can we do to help, sir?"

Ivers finished off his scotch.

"We have a saboteur destroying Walt Disney World, attraction by attraction. First *Tiki Room*. Then *Stitch*. Now *Carousel of Progress*. Who knows what's next? Charlie, you say Reginald here isn't the culprit. That may be true, but he's certainly an accessory to the crime."

"Man, I haven't sabotaged jack shit, and I haven't helped anyone sabotage jack shit," said Habst.

"Oh, but you have. You have indeed helped the perpetrator of these crimes greatly."

"And how exactly do you figure that?"

"Detective," said Ivers, turning to Charlie. "Care to venture a guess?"

"Oh no," said Charlie, after thinking for a few seconds. "Oh, Habst. How did I miss this? The videos!"

"Excellent deduction! That's absolutely correct. It's your videos, Reginald. He's using your backstage videos to plan his sabotage."

"Oh shit," said Habst.

"Oh shit, indeed," said Ivers.

"Dammit!" yelled Charlie, smacking the table. "*Tiki* and *Stitch*. They both happened right after Habst posted his videos. But they were too far apart from each other. I didn't even consider it. But then *Carousel*…. Twice is a coincidence, three times is a pattern. How did I not see the pattern?"

"Getting rusty, eh, Charlie?" asked Ivers.

Charlie shook his head, and looked at Habst.

"I got personally involved with the main suspect. Classic mistake."

"To be fair, Burbank didn't figure it out until all hell broke loose in *Carousel* the day after Reginald was arrested in there. After that, it wasn't hard to connect the dots. And, to be honest, my boys got it wrong. They just assumed Reginald had committed the sabotages himself."

"Ooooh shiiiiit," said Habst.

"I think you've already clearly expressed that sentiment," said Ivers.

"I know who's been doing this. I mean, I don't actually know, but I know. Damn, man. Damn."

"That was illuminating," said Ivers.

"Look, here's the deal. A few years ago, some dude named

Sat-Com messaged me on a hacker forum. He'd seen my backstage vids, had a request for more, and was willing to pay me in virtcoins for them. I figured, 'Hell, I'm going to film this stuff anyway, so why not get paid for it?' So I filmed what he wanted, uploaded it, and got my virtcoins. I never figured the guy was going to use the videos to sabotage stuff. I just figured he was curious about how the 'magic' was made, or some nonsense like that, just like the other subscribers to my channel."

"Christ, Habst!" yelled Charlie. "What if this guy is a terrorist? What if he'd used your videos to kill people? Did you ever think of that? You'd be an accessory to a terrorist attack!"

"Damn," said Habst. "It never even crossed my mind. I swear."

"This is a very interesting development," said Ivers, leaning back in his chair. "Reginald, what do you know about this person?"

"Nothing. Nothing at all. He just asks me for videos, and I get paid. He's very specific about what he wants. Uh… and he refers to himself as 'we', which I always thought was strange."

"Dammit!" said Charlie. "So there really could be some sort of organized group behind this. Not good. Has he ever expressed any sort of political agenda, or said anything with religious connotations, or anything like that?"

"Nope. He just says 'good job' and sends me my virtcoins. He bailed me out of jail, too, which was cool."

"So that's your good old Uncle Walt?" asked Charlie. "Thanks for being so straight with me, Habst."

"Whatever, man. Before I knew all of this stuff, I didn't think it was relevant, okay? Plus, I didn't want to rat him out. The dude has always kept his promises, he's always paid me quickly, and he's always been very appreciative of my work. That's better treatment than I got when I worked Custodial at Disney."

Ivers leaned into the table and locked onto Habst with a steely gaze.

"Let's cut the shit," he said. "I've got a potential PR nightmare on my hands here. Nobody is going to visit the Magic Kingdom if they think they're going to get blown up. I'm already having a hell of a time keeping a lid on this thing. We can't even file a damned insurance claim yet; without solid evidence of sabotage, they'll demand a safety investigation, and we'll get torn apart for code violations. The Feds are snooping around, and I'm throwing piles of cash at local reporters to keep them from going public. If the Associated Press gets wind of this, the stock will take a nosedive, and the Board will be out for blood. And you two will be the ones who take the fall, because I sure as hell am not coming out of this looking anything less than sparkling clean."

He turned to Charlie.

"You're the head of Security here. You've failed at your job. You'll be fired and your name will be dragged through the mud. You'll have trouble getting a job as a police chief in Mayberry."

He turned to Habst.

"And you. Our legal team will throw the book at you. Did you see the list of charges that have already been filed?"

Habst nodded.

"Well that's nothing. That list will triple. At least. Hell, I wouldn't be surprised to see a murder charge on there at the end of the day. And believe me when I say that every last charge will stick. Our lawyers eat idiots like you for breakfast and shit them out before lunch. You will be sent to prison, and you will never, ever get out."

Habst gulped.

"So. Charlie. Reginald. Here's what's going to happen. You're going to find this guy, and you're going to bring him down. I don't care how you do it, but I want this guy out of the picture. Permanently. Throw him off the top of Cinderella's

Castle for all I care. Just deal with the situation before he has a chance to do any further damage."

"Cinderella Castle," said Habst.

"Jesus, Habst," said Charlie.

"Excuse me?" said Ivers.

"It's Cinderella… never mind."

"I don't like you, Reginald," said Ivers. "I think you're an arrogant little prick."

"The feeling is mutual."

"I'm sure it is. But I'm a man of my word. You sort this out within the next three days, and all charges will be dropped. We'll even pay off that Purcelli lady so she shuts up about her precious daughter and doesn't lose her house. And Charlie, you can expect a handsome raise."

He stood up and smoothed out his jacket.

"Gentlemen, do we have an understanding?"

"We sure do, Mr. Ivers," said Charlie.

"Reginald?"

"I mean, yeah, I guess."

"Excellent. You have three days, boys."

Ivers walked out of the bar, followed by his two thugs. He stopped, and turned around.

"Looking forward to that game of golf, Charlie," he said, and continued walking.

"What a dick," said Habst.

"No argument here," said Charlie.

They walked out of the resort, got in the car, and drove in uncomfortable silence.

Habst farted loudly.

"Sorry," said Habst, rolling down the window. "I'm having some major stomach issues. That goddamned scotch didn't help."

Charlie laughed.

"Ever heard of laxatives?"

"Man, screw that. I don't got time to be sitting on a toilet all day."

"Better than being constipated."

Habst groaned.

"It's starting to seem that way, yeah."

Charlie looked over at him for a second, and then turned back to the road.

"You've really screwed me over big time, Habst. You know that?"

"I know."

"You've endangered my livelihood, and the well-being of my family. How am I going to afford college tuition for the girls if I don't have a job?"

"I'm sorry. I'll figure something out. I'll make it better somehow. I promise."

Charlie smiled and patted him on the leg.

"I know you're not a bad guy, Habst. I know you have good intentions. You're just really bad at life."

"You can say that again."

"So let's try to work out a plan to get out of this mess before we get back home and I get the third degree from Meghan."

"Okay, I'm pumped. Let's go."

"Well, first things first, you need to get in touch with this guy. What does he call himself? Sat-Com? What does that mean?"

"Beats me. Satellite Communications? And it doesn't really work like that. He gets in touch with me. I've tried hitting him up for jobs when I was running low on weed, and I never got any response."

"It's worth a shot, though."

"Yeah, I guess. But we don't want to spook him."

"Good point."

"I guess I can just tell him that I got kicked out of my place and I need some quick cash."

"Okay, and then what?"

"And then hopefully he offers me another job. He said he

had something huge coming up in the next few days."

"That doesn't sound good."

"It sounded awesome at the time. Now, not so much."

When they got back to the house, Habst powered on his laptop and connected to the Tor network.

"What's going on?" asked Meghan. "How did the meeting with Bill Ivers go?"

"Terrible," said Charlie.

"What's he doing?" she said, noticing Habst typing frantically.

"God help us… he's trying to save us all."

# TWENTY-TWO

I T TOOK THEM ABOUT a half hour of constant bickering to work up a suitably non-suspicious message for Sat-Com:

*Thanks for paying my bail. Lots of charges against me, though. I think I'll be going to prison for a while. If you want me to do another job, now's the time. I'd like to have some cash to settle up my affairs before I get put away.*

Habst sent it, and then they waited. For the first hour, they just stood around his laptop, staring at his inbox, refreshing it occasionally. At midnight, Meghan went to bed. An hour later, Charlie gave up.

"I told you, Charlie. The dude works on his own schedule. We'll just have to wait for him to get in touch."

"It's infuriating. I hate it when people have something over me."

"Like Bill Ivers?"

"Yeah. Like Bill Ivers."

"It must suck to work for such a prick."

"He's a shrewd businessman. But he doesn't give a damn about the parks or the employees or Walt Disney's legacy. All he cares about is the stock price, and how big of a bonus he'll get at the end of each year."

"So why are you working for him?"

"Because he owed me one, and because I wanted the girls to grow up with happy memories of Walt Disney World. I didn't want them to think of Florida as the place where they were kidnapped, their mother was beaten within an inch of her life, and their father killed a bunch of people. And, to be honest, I needed an easy job with minimal stress and not a lot of danger. Which was exactly what I had until you started causing trouble."

"Yeah…. I honestly do feel bad about all of this. Hell, I've felt bad about bugging you for a while now. I've always had a lot of respect for you. But between my curiosity and the money he was throwing at me, I just couldn't turn down those video jobs."

"Well, if it wasn't you, it would've been someone else. Sat-Com seems to have a plan, and is pretty determined to see it through. At least he picked someone who loves the parks and who has some shred of decency and morality."

"I don't know about all of that."

"I do. You're a good guy, beneath all of the idiocy."

"Wow, now I know what to put on my tombstone."

Charlie laughed and stood up.

"I'm going to bed. If he gets in touch, wake me up."

"Will do. I'll probably take a sip of the vaporizer and then hit the sack myself."

"Don't set the house on fire."

"I won't. That's a promise."

"G'night, Habst."

"Night, Charlie."

Charlie left the room, and Habst stood, picked up his laptop, and went into the guest bedroom. He propped up some pillows and laid on the bed, setting the laptop next to him, and pulled his weed and the vaporizer out of his safe.

It was strange for him, sleeping in a nice bed with clean crisp sheets, smoking his vaporizer, and not having Monika there. He wondered if she'd ever forgive him. He hoped so.

He really liked her. She was smart, she picked locks, she was gorgeous, and she didn't mind that he was a hopeless bum. He liked those qualities in a girl.

He started nodding off. He pulled himself up in the bed, took a final puff off the vaporizer, and reached over to turn off the nightstand lamp. Realizing he'd left his laptop powered on and sitting next to him, he flipped up the lid and checked his HackNCrackBB messages a final time.

He had one new message.

"Oh crap!"

He opened it, fully intending to yell for Charlie, until he read the first line.

*We know you're staying with Charlie Walker.*

"Uh oh."

*Charlie Walker is a fine man. An honorable man. He seems to have a deep respect for the parks. But he cannot be allowed to interfere with our mission.*

"Dammit."

*Our offer is for one final shoot. One thousand virtcoins. ALL charges against you will be dropped. Charlie will keep his job. Nobody will be harmed. But only if you act alone. We're watching you. We will know if Charlie gets involved. We've always followed through with our promises, and we're asking you to trust us one final time.*

Habst didn't like this at all. He'd continually deceived Charlie, and had finally realized how wrong that had been. It didn't seem possible that Sat-Com could know Charlie was in the loop, but then again, it didn't seem possible that he could do any of the crazy stuff he'd already done.

Plus, one thousand virtcoins was an outrageous amount of money: over one hundred thousand dollars. That was enough to enable him to be self-sufficient for the first time in years. He could start a new life. Stop being a bum. Make Charlie and Monika proud.

So, who did he trust to make things right for him and

Charlie? That jerk Bill Ivers who didn't give a damn about anything other than covering his own ass, or Sat-Com, who'd always done right by him?

Except that Sat-Com was trying to destroy the parks. Walt's parks.

*You keep destroying attractions,* wrote Habst. *Crappy attractions, but still. I can't be a part of the destruction of Walt Disney World.*

*Ivers is destroying the parks, not us,* came the reply. *We're trying to save them, and you can help. Please believe that. Our reasons will become clear soon enough.*

Habst didn't buy it. But there was nothing stopping him from accepting Sat-Com's deal. Ivers didn't need to know. If Sat-Com turned out to be a worse jerk than Ivers, he'd just switch sides, capture Sat-Com, and deliver him to Ivers as per the original plan.

*Okay, you've got a deal. What do you need?*

*Full monorail ride–thru from TTC to Epcot from inside the cockpit. Need to see all controls. Close-ups of the Leave a Legacy tombstones, focusing on their bases. Interior of the Mission: SPACE Orange simulator bay. Need a full wide-angle loop of the complete ride from outside of the centrifuges. Finally, backstage at Imagination, especially the maintenance bay.*

Habst had no idea how he was going to get some of these shots. The Mission: SPACE one in particular would be nearly impossible to film. The simulator bays had pressure mats on the floor and at least a dozen cameras pointing everywhere, and the centrifuges wouldn't even start if the entire bay wasn't completely clear of people. Also, there was no way he was going to be able to spend any time in the Imagination maintenance bay without a Cast Member ID and some sort of uniform. Finally, apart from the pilots, nobody had been allowed in the monorail cockpits since 2009, when a twenty-one-year-old pilot had been killed in a horrible accident.

*Sure. No problem.*

*Great. Can you have the videos uploaded by this afternoon?*

"Not a chance in hell," said Habst.

*You bet.*

*Excellent. Virtcoins will be delivered once our mission is complete. Charges against you will be dropped at the same time, and Charlie Walker will be notified that his job is secure. If our mission fails because you've tipped somebody off, you will receive nothing, you will go to jail, and Charlie Walker will lose his job.*

*Got it.*

*Trust us, Habst. We got you into this mess, and we'll get you out. You might not believe it now, but we're the good guys.*

"Yeah, because good guys just love blackmailing people," said Habst.

*I believe you.*

*Good. Get some sleep. You have a big day ahead of you.*

*10-4.*

Habst deleted the conversation, closed the lid of the laptop, and sat on the bed, thinking. He sat there until dawn, desperately trying to figure out a plan of action.

And what he came up with was so outrageous, so completely off the wall, that there was no way it could possibly work.

"Eh, at least it'll be a good final adventure before they lock me up for the rest of my life," he said.

# Twenty-Three

Any word from Sat-Com?" asked Charlie, shaking Habst awake a mere thirty minutes after he'd fallen asleep.

"Huh?"

"Sat-Com!"

"Oh," he said, rubbing his eyes. "Uh, let me check."

He opened the lid of his laptop and refreshed the mailbox.

"Nope. Nothing yet."

"Damn. We only have two days left to take him down. Can you send him another message?"

Habst yawned.

"No way, Charlie. He'll know something is up if I seem too desperate. All he knows now is that I need some cash. He has no idea we're onto him."

"Right. I just hate the waiting."

"Me too. I think I'm gonna pass the time by visiting Monika again. Pull a Charlie Walker and stake the place out until her mother leaves. Maybe I can talk some sense into her without that crazy bitch around."

"Not a bad plan. You'll keep checking your messages?"

"Sure. Every thirty minutes."

"That works. And you'll call me as soon as you hear something?"

"Yeah, of course."

"Okay. Good luck with Monika."

"Thanks…. Hey, where are Meghan and the kids?"

"Meghan had an early class to teach, and the kids are at school. Life goes on."

"Is she okay?"

"She's worried, but she trusts us to make sure everything turns out okay."

"By 'us', I assume you mean 'you'?"

"No, Habst. She trusts you, too."

"Wow."

"Yeah. She's obviously nuts."

Habst's stomach tensed. This whole situation was not helping his constipation.

"Oh, hey, do you have a bike I could borrow? I left mine at Monika's house."

Charlie paused. A smile slowly crept across his face.

"I've got a bike for you, but you're not going to like it."

They walked out to the garage and Charlie flipped on the light.

"There she is!" said Charlie, pointing to a bright-pink ten-speed with a yellow banana seat, a wicker basket, a bell, and fluorescent blue streamers attached to the handlebars.

"Aw, c'mon, man!"

"Isn't she a beauty? Katie calls it Ghost Rider."

"That doesn't make any sense. Ghost Rider has a flaming motorcycle."

"Yeah, I explained that to her."

"I can't be seen riding this thing."

"Well, that's all we've got. So it's either this, or you're hoofing it."

"Lend me your car."

"You don't even have a license!"

"Man!"

"Don't you dare put a scratch on this bike. Katie would not

be pleased. And I'm pretty sure you wouldn't stand a chance against her."

"Yeah, she could probably kick my ass."

"Most likely."

"Damn. Fine. Can I get a key to the house in case I get shot down by Monika? I'm gonna need some place to charge the laptop."

"Sure."

Charlie walked out of the garage. Habst hopped on the bike and howled in pain as the banana seat crushed his testicles.

"You have to ride it like a horse!" said Charlie, coming back into the garage. He handed Habst a key. Habst grabbed it and shoved it into his pocket.

"I don't know how to ride a goddamned horse!"

"Put your weight on the stirrups, not the saddle."

"What?"

"Don't sit on the seat, stand on the pedals."

"Oh."

Charlie opened the garage door. Habst picked up his backpack, got on the bike, and, following Charlie's instructions, pedaled out of the garage without harming his family jewels.

"See ya, Charlie!" he said, riding off.

"Good luck!" yelled Charlie, and closed the garage door.

Habst turned the corner and rode off the street into a wooded area near an empty lot. He pulled out his cell phone and dialed 911.

"Hi. I'd like to report a suspicious guy walking around the Magic Kingdom. I just saw him go into Pirates of the Caribbean with a backpack, and when he came out he didn't have the backpack anymore. He was talking to himself and acting all sketchy. I'd like to remain anonymous. Bye."

Habst hung up the phone and hid behind a bush. Two minutes later, Charlie Walker's Camry shot across the intersection, going at least sixty miles per hour.

He rode back to the house, unlocked the back door, and

spent the next fifteen minutes ransacking the place. He finally found his Cast Member ID in the last place he'd think to look: the vegetable drawer of the refrigerator.

"Clever bastard," said Habst.

Before he left, he also took a battery-powered drill from the garage, a pair of night-vision glasses from Charlie's closet, a tube of toothpaste from the bathroom, a straw from the kitchen, and some Sticky Tack that was holding up a poster of Jack Sparrow in Katie's room. He put them all into his backpack.

"Sorry, Charlie," he said, locking the backdoor and pedaling off to Walt Disney World.

---

"WHAT DO YOU MEAN you didn't find any backpack?" yelled Charlie. "Dammit, bring up the security camera footage from the queue."

Charlie scanned the footage and saw nobody with a backpack enter the ride building around the time of the call.

"Run a trace on the number that reported the bomb."

"Already did that, sir. The number is registered to Reginald Habstermeister."

"Habst?! Oh no."

Charlie slumped into his chair.

"What is that idiot planning now?"

# TWENTY-FOUR

THE BIKE WAS ACTUALLY pretty nice once he got the hang of it. Habst was used to his old rusty dirt bike that had three working gears and non-functional front brakes. If he got those virtcoins, the first thing he was going to do was get a new bike.

Or he could learn to drive a car.

He laughed. That was pure nonsense and he knew it. He had trouble steering his way around the Tomorrowland Speedway track.

He pulled into the Buena Vista Place apartments, carefully stashed the bike in some thick bushes, and walked across the road to the Cast Member lot. He put his fake ID around his neck and took the bus to the park, happy that the air conditioning was working.

The bus stopped, and he got off and headed to Costuming.

He sidled up to the counter and handed over his ID.

"I need a Custodial uniform."

The Cast Member behind the counter swiped his ID and handed it back to him.

"You sure about that?" she asked.

"Yeah. Why?"

"Says here you're the Vice President of Human Resources

for the whole resort."

"Uh…. Yeah, well, I like to get my hands dirty and mingle with the front-line Cast Members a few times a week. See what their working conditions are like, listen to any complaints, eat in their cafeteria. I'm cool like that."

"I've never seen you down here before."

"You must be new."

"I've been here sixteen years."

"You've been here sixteen years and you're still down in the basement doling out costumes?! Shouldn't you be a manager by now or something?"

"You tell me, Mr. Vice President."

"Have you at least applied for other positions?"

"Sure. A ton. They always seem to go to someone's stupid relative."

"Ah, good old nepotism. Personally, I hate my family, so…."

"So, does that mean you'll help me?"

"What's your name?"

"Tricia Meyers."

"Well, Tricia, if you can do me a big favor and get me a nice clean Custodial outfit, I'll see what I can do."

Tricia left and came back a minute later with a cleanly pressed uniform.

"Thanks for the uniform, Tricia," said Habst, "and thank you greatly for your years of service."

Habst grabbed his uniform and headed to the nearest locker room. It was just after the three o'clock parade, and the locker room was full of sweaty face and fur characters.

"Gross," said Habst.

He pulled his shirt and jeans off, folded them carefully, and stuffed them in his backpack.

"Oooh, fresh meat," said a young kid who had just taken off a Peter Pan costume. The boy headed into the shower and turned back to Habst. "Curtain half open means anyone is free to enter."

Peter Pan walked into the shower, leaving the curtain parted halfway. Habst looked at the other shower curtains. They were all parted halfway.

Habst quickly threw on his Custodial outfit.

"Remember, boys," shouted Habst. "Walt Disney said that water conservation was an important part of the future of urban living! So do your part to conserve water, and shower together!"

He ran out of the locker room, snickering, as eight Cast Members stuck their heads out of their shower stalls, noticed the half-open shower curtains, looked at each other, smiled, and started doubling and tripling up.

Habst walked down the Utilidors towards Main Street, and headed up the stairs to the East Parking lot. He walked out of the lot, crossed back over to the front of the park, and got on a monorail to the Ticket and Transportation Center.

After a few minutes the monorail arrived at the TTC. The doors swished open, and he exited and went down the ramp.

He walked around the huge structure until he reached the Custodial supply room. He opened the door and grabbed a mop, a bucket, and a yellow 'Caution: Wet Floor' sign. He put his backpack into the bucket, put the mop on top of it, closed the door, and took the ramp up to the TTC's Epcot platform.

He opened the gate at the end of the waiting area and walked up to the attendant standing at the head of the station.

"Big crowd," he said, looking at the line of people waiting in line. "Got a report of an incoming Code V in the front car." He moved closer to her. "Apparently someone started changing their kid's diaper in there. Packed full, and someone's changing a diaper. Off-duty CM called it in."

"You're kidding me," said the attendant.

"Wish I was, wish I was. Look, I know we got a full house here, but I'd really appreciate it if you'd just not load that front car. I could do a rush job on the cleanup, but who knows what we've got in there? A smell like that in a confined space, and next thing you know, everyone is puking. The whole car could be covered in vomit! Don't want to try to clean that up in a rush. Want to give it a nice scrub down, you know?"

The attendant nodded in disgust.

"So let's just not load that car, huh? I'll head in there as soon as it's empty. That'll give me a good ten minutes to get it all spick and span before it shows up at Epcot. Deal?"

"You take your job way too seriously."

"Monorails are the transportation of the future," said Habst. "And the future isn't supposed to smell like dirty diapers."

"Whatever," said the attendant.

The monorail pulled up to the station. Instead of the clean and sleek look it normally sported, this one was covered in a "wrap": a big sticker used as a temporary paint job. This particular wrap was advertising *Duffy: The Movie*. Duffy was a beige teddy bear that Disney had fabricated solely to sell stuffed animals, outfits for those stuffed animals, and now, apparently, movies. The bear had zero personality and his design was painfully generic.

*Goddamned Duffy*, thought Habst.

The monorail doors opened and the cars unloaded. Habst ran into the front car with the mop and bucket, and stood up the Wet Floor sign in front of the door.

"Oh lordy!" he said, poking his head out and holding his nose. "What a mess!"

The attendant nodded and directed the waiting Guests to the other cars.

Habst quickly pulled his backpack out of the bucket, removed the portable drill, and put in a quarter-inch drill bit. As soon as the doors closed, he started drilling midway down the wall closest to the cockpit.

"Sorry, Walt," he said, as bits of plastic flew everywhere. Seconds later, he'd drilled a hole clear through the wall. The constant radio jabbering in the cockpit was loud enough that the pilot hadn't heard anything.

Habst put down the drill, pulled out his phone, started recording, and pushed the lens against the hole. He looked at the screen, adjusted the angle accordingly, and zoomed in on the control panel. The shot was perfect.

The monorail started moving, and for ten minutes he filmed everything that the pilot touched on the central control panel. The kid was a pro, maintaining his speed through each checkpoint, keeping a sharp lookout for obstacles on the track, and joking with dispatch the whole time over the radio.

As Habst listened to the pilot and watched him on the phone's screen, he thought of the young Cast Member who had died in the cab of Monorail Purple a few years before. Through no fault of his own the kid had been crushed to death when another monorail had backed into his cab. Turned out a switch hadn't been thrown to divert the other monorail to the maintenance bay. The pilot of that monorail had no idea; the protocol of moving the pilot to the rear cab when backing up had long since been abandoned, and the side view mirrors were absolutely useless around a curve, or in the fog, or in the dark, or pretty much in any adverse conditions.

By the time the pilot of that monorail realized what was happening, it was too late. He had already plowed into the front cab of the monorail sitting at the TTC station.

The worst part was that the young pilot at the TTC had seen the other monorail coming towards him, and had tried to put his train in reverse. But he simply didn't have enough time. The thought of him knowing, even for a few seconds, that the vehicle that he loved so much was about to kill him was horrifying to Habst.

He could just imagine sitting in that cab, and seeing the nose of the other monorail coming at him in slow motion. The cone bursting through the windows, shards of Plexiglas shooting through his skin. The tip of the train pushing against the control console, breaking it free of its bolts and forcing it slowly forward. The thick steel crushing his legs, and then pushing into his ribcage, breaking through his lungs and heart. Seeing his own blood covering the thing he'd loved most at Walt Disney World, the vehicle he'd always dreamed of piloting… and knowing for those few awful moments that something had gone horribly wrong, and that his dream had turned into a nightmare.

Habst had read the NTSB reports, and he knew that the accident never would have happened if there had been a pilot in the rear cab, which used to be standard procedure, but which was stopped to save time and money.

The accident never would have happened if the manager on duty had someone to relieve him for his lunch break, but budget cutbacks had reduced staff to a skeleton crew.

The accident never would have happened if the overworked switch operator had double-checked his work, but he was new and undertrained, and nobody was there to look over his shoulder.

In short, the accident never should have happened, but budget cuts called for by upper management, starting and ending with Bill Ivers, had killed a young man whose main happiness in life was driving a goddamned monorail.

Habst hated Bill Ivers.

As soon as the monorail had pulled into the Epcot station, Habst stopped recording and started uploading the video to YouTube, granting only Sat-Com viewing rights. He then swept up all of the plastic pieces that had come off the wall and dumped them in the mop bucket.

He pulled the straw and the tube of toothpaste out of his backpack. He filled the straw with the white paste and slowly blew it into the hole in the monorail wall. Once the hole was filled, he squeezed more toothpaste onto his finger and rubbed it across the hole until it was perfectly flush.

It wasn't a perfect blend, and it certainly wouldn't look great on the pilot's side, but it was good enough that nobody would notice for a few days.

He threw his backpack into the bucket and put the mop on top of it. The doors opened, and Habst walked out.

"Whew!" he said to that station's attendant. "That was a mess, let me tell you!"

He grabbed the yellow sign and rolled the mop bucket into the elevator, took it to the bottom of the station, went into a Custodial closet, and closed the door. Inside, he changed out of his uniform and back into his street clothes, carefully folding the outfit before putting it in his backpack.

Stepping out of the room, he put his ID on, and hung a right at the main entrance towards The Seas. Next to the Guest Services building was a door, which he opened. On the other side of the door was a switchback. He wove through the switchback, and was backstage. Just past the Guest Services building was a bus circle, and beyond that was a path which led to another switchback that opened out just past the bathrooms beside the park's iconic ride and architectural weenie, Spaceship Earth. He walked onstage, took his ID off, doubled back towards the main courtyard, and was greeted with a sight of dozens of huge granite tombstones.

"Ugh," he said.

The Leave a Legacy monuments were a cash grab; a marketing opportunity the likes of which had never been seen before in a Disney park. On each ugly granite slab were hundreds of miniscule pictures of people who had paid their hard-earned money to be immortalized in Epcot. Except the whole idea was so poorly executed that even if you knew exactly where your picture was located, you'd still be hard pressed to find it, and if you did, you'd be hard pressed to recognize your family in the grainy low-res black-and-white picture.

None of this would have been so bad if the monuments had been placed outside the park, or had been designed to match the futuristic aesthetic of the main courtyard. Instead, they clashed with the gorgeous and massive Spaceship Earth, which obliterated any sense of proportion or scale that the design of the Leave a Legacy rocks hoped to convey.

In short, they looked like huge tombstones. A depressing and almost apocalyptic talisman in the entrance of a park created to celebrate the future and inspire people to strive for a better world. But walking through the gates and being greeted with cold, ugly, depressing memorials to families with too much expendable cash was more likely to produce feelings of dread and depression than hope and excitement.

Habst circled around the tombstones with his phone, starting with a wide shot of the whole mess. There were two columns and six rows, with one column on either side of a huge planter that was centered in front of Spaceship Earth. Each row was broken up in an irregular pattern, and the pattern was not symmetrical across the columns. In short, it was a total mess of a design. Habst did his best to document the layout, paying particular attention to the bases of the slabs, per Sat-Com's instructions.

Once he was done shooting them, he started another upload to YouTube and began the long walk to Mission: SPACE. It was extremely hot outside, and the walk was not pleasant. There was a reason that people joked EPCOT stood for "Every Person Comes Out Tired".

He finally reached Mission: SPACE, a vomit-inducing ride that simulated a spaceflight to Mars, complete with the experience of extra G-forces that made your cheeks pull back, just like in the old astronaut training videos. Habst had been on the ride a few times and didn't care for it. He didn't like that the story of the ride couldn't seem to make up its mind whether you were actually supposed to be taking a trip to Mars, or whether the whole thing was supposed to be a simulation. He was also still pissed that they'd torn down the totally amazing Horizons to build this vastly inferior attraction.

Habst had to admit that the simulated G-force was an impressive technological feat. He had no idea how they did it, but he'd find out soon enough.

He walked through the queue, listened to Lieutenant Dan's annoying spiels, and was ushered into a large room that contained ten simulator pods. Each pod contained four seats. He was assigned to a pod with two other riders, a lady and a man. They sat at one end, and he sat at the other end, leaving an empty seat between them.

Habst stuck his phone out of the pod and snapped a picture of the gray wall behind it.

"I don't know about this, Mark," said the lady at the end of the pod to the man sitting next to her. "You know I have a weak stomach."

"I'm sure you'll be fine, Lucy," said Mark. "Disney wouldn't put a ride in Epcot that made people puke, right?"

"I've been on this ride a million times," said Habst, butting in. "They say that if you start to feel sick, don't look straight at the screen. Instead, you should turn your head from side to side to get reoriented."

This was absolutely incorrect, and Habst knew it. It was best to focus as hard as possible on the screen in front of you, since the movement of the ride was timed to coincide with the footage on the screens.

"Worst case, just use this," said Habst, pointing to a vomit bag.

"Thanks," said Lucy, staring at the bag.

"No problem!"

The pod door closed, and in a few seconds the countdown for the liftoff to Mars began.

Habst, ignoring the countdown completely, set the screensaver of his phone to the solid gray picture of the wall that he'd just taken. He then set the camera to record out of the screen-side lens, and put it back in his pocket.

As the liftoff commenced, the G-forces in the pod increased greatly, and Lucy groaned. Habst looked over at her.

"Side to side!" he yelled.

She did what he said, and immediately turned as white as

a sheet.

Habst let out a horrible fart that he'd been holding for at least an hour.

"Oh god!" yelled Lucy. She pulled out the vomit bag and puked into it repeatedly. The G-forces increased again, and some of the vomit from the bag flew back into her face and splattered Mark.

"Aw, that's a shame," said Habst.

Finally, the ride ended. Lucy's head was covered in vomit, and Mark had a fair amount on him. Habst had avoided the spray, but the combined smell of his fart and the vomit was making him feel a bit queasy.

The door to the simulator opened, and they all stumbled out.

"Christ," said Habst, gasping for air.

He motioned to the Cast Member standing by the exit.

"There's a lot of puke in there, man."

The Cast Member stuck his head into the simulator and immediately yanked it back in disgust. He pulled out his radio.

"We have a Code V in Bay Three Orange."

As the Cast Member was speaking on the radio and assessing the damage in the simulator, Habst pulled his phone out of his pocket, started recording, locked the phone so the screensaver of the gray wall displayed on the screen, and walked behind the simulators closest to the exit. He pulled the Sticky Tack out of his pocket, tore off a few small pieces, stuck them to the back of the phone, and quickly stuck the phone against the wall, about a foot off the floor and with a clear view between two simulator pods into the center of the room. The screensaver blended perfectly with the gray wall behind it. The slight reflectivity of the glass dampened the illusion a bit, but he hoped nobody would notice. And if you looked at it from the side the matte black finish of the phone made it appear to be a junction box or motion sensor, or some other sort of machinery that was supposed to be there.

Habst walked out of the simulator bay, smiling and waving to Mark and Lucy, who were sitting on a bench in the hallway, covered in vomit and looking miserable.

"Enjoy your day!" said Habst.

He left the ride building, waited five minutes, which was the amount of time he figured the Cast Members would spend cleaning the puke from the simulator, and then circled back to the entrance. As usual, the line for the ride was practically non-existent, so he moved through the queue quickly.

He then stood off to the side of the line, pretending to work up the nerve to go on it, until the simulator bay he was in previously started loading. He glanced at the wall, verified that his phone was still stuck to it, got into his designated simulator, and went through the entire ride again.

At the end, he got out of the car, feigned nausea, and stumbled to his phone. He bent over, acting like he might puke, pulled the phone off the wall, shoved it in his pocket, and quickly walked out of the bay, holding his stomach.

Once outside, Habst pulled the phone out, stopped it from recording, removed the Sticky Tack, and replayed the video. It was fascinating. The individual simulator pods were all mounted from above to long arms that were attached to a huge column in the middle of the room. At certain times during the ride, whenever the rider was meant to experience G-forces, the column would start rotating faster and faster until all ten simulators attached to it were spinning so fast that they just looked like a big blur. The individual pods also pivoted backwards and forwards at specific times to match the movement of the footage playing inside. It was an impressive engineering job, to be sure.

But the ride still sucked.

Habst started uploading the Mission: SPACE footage and made the lengthy trek to the abandoned Odyssey restaurant. The restaurant had been closed for years, but they kept the bathrooms open. However, just like the Tomorrowland

Terrace in the Magic Kingdom, since nobody ever went to the restaurant, nobody ever went into the bathrooms, either.

Predictably, they were empty. He pulled the Custodial outfit from his backpack, quickly changed into it, and put his Cast Member ID on.

Yet again, Habst had to traverse a long distance to get from the Odyssey in Future World East all the way over to Future World West, which is where the Imagination pavilion was located. Taking out his phone, he hit record, and held it casually by his side. He walked straight past the front of the pavilion, noting that, as usual, there was no line for the ride inside.

Probably because it, like Mission: SPACE, sucked.

The original incarnation of the ride was amazing, with the purple dragon Figment's creator, Dreamfinder, guiding the rider through a magical world of make-believe whimsy. But in 1998 it had been gutted, shortened, and dumbed down, with Eric Idle taking over Dreamfinder's role as the attraction's guide. Figment was gone, too, and with him went the soul of the ride.

Habst loved Eric Idle and was a huge Monty Python fan, but his role in the refurbished ride was that of a total buzzkilling dick. He did the best he could with an awful script, but, damn, if Eric Idle couldn't save a show, then you knew it was a total crap fest.

Eventually, after a huge number of Guest complaints, Figment was added back into the ride. But he wasn't the same. It was like he'd been permanently scarred by his exile, and was now a sarcastic, jaded asshole who just wanted to cause trouble and mess with Eric Idle and the Guests, to the point where he actually farted on people.

Journey Into Imagination With Figment was a terrible attraction, and Habst hated riding it because he felt like he was giving his implicit support to mediocrity. He also felt like he was trampling all over the grave of a ride that had given him, and countless others, so many happy childhood memories.

Habst walked past the pavilion and through a switchback that led backstage. He continued walking past some parking spots and a few trailers, and then made a left, following a path that wrapped around the exterior of the building. Finally, he reached the maintenance bay and entered the huge room.

On the right were a set of industrial machines designed to clean and sterilize the 3D glasses used for *Captain EO*. Two racks of dirty glasses were stacked up next to the cleaning station, but there was nobody manning the machines. Probably for the best, as he didn't need people standing around, asking him questions.

He continued towards the back of the room, where a piece of track curved from around a corner and then dead-ended in the middle of the bay. There was a ride vehicle sitting on it, and he realized it was the maintenance spur, a section of track that split off from the main ride so that damaged vehicles could be taken out of rotation and fixed without needing to lift them out with a crane.

Habst stepped under the track and examined the underside of the vehicle, filming everything he saw. The core of the vehicle was attached to thick iron machinery that looked complicated, rugged, and very heavy.

"Son, now just what the hell are you doing under there?" asked an old man.

Habst jolted up, hit his head on the track, and walked out from under the ride vehicle. He casually slipped his phone into his pocket.

"That hurt," said Habst, rubbing the back of his head and examining the man.

He looked to be in his mid-sixties, with white hair and a deeply wrinkled face. He was wearing dirty blue coveralls and had a filthy red shop rag sticking of his front pocket. His name tag said, simply, "Jenkins".

"You shouldn't be back here," said Jenkins. "Liable to get

yourself killed around all this heavy machinery."

"They told me to come here and find Jenkins."

"I'm Jenkins, dammit! Who told you to find me?"

"Ride Ops. Called in a Custodial emergency on car three, train B."

"A Custodial emergency? What in God's name is that?"

"Beats me. They wouldn't say it over the radio. Must be pretty bad."

"Well what the hell do they want me to do about it?"

"Pull that car off the track, I guess."

"Pull one car off the track for a Custodial emergency?! Ha!"

Jenkins started laughing. Big huge guffaws roared out of his mouth.

"Haha," said Habst.

"Take one car off the track for Custodial! That's a good one!" said Jenkins, still laughing.

"Yeah…. So…. I'm guessing that's a problem?"

Jenkins slapped Habst across back of his head.

"Dammit, boy, don't you got no sense in that head of yours?"

"Ow!"

"Bunch of idiots working in Ride Ops these days. Apparently nobody knows how these damn things work anymore except Jenkins here! Good old Jenkins, still getting paid jack shit after thirty-one years fixing this beast. Yeah, sure, let me just wave my hands and make number three on train B magically appear."

He waved his hands around. Nothing happened.

"Nothing happened," said Habst.

"Of course nothing happened, you fool! You know how long it takes to get a single car into this bay? A good hour!"

"I don't understand."

"'Course you don't. Nobody does. Look, you follow me, and then you go back and tell those idiots in Ride Ops exactly what you seen here, okay?"

"Uh, okay. You mind if I film this so I can show them

instead of just telling them?"

"Good idea. Film away."

Habst pulled his phone out of his pocket and followed Jenkins down the length of the track. The room gradually got darker the further they walked.

Jenkins slightly parted a black curtain that draped over the track. It opened onto a bright scene filled with an orange sky, clouds, and Figment hanging from the ceiling in various places. He pointed past the curtain into the darkness.

"There's the fork."

A string of four red ride cars coasted through the scene. As they passed, Habst could see the outline of the track, and the place where it split off.

"Okay, I see it."

"And here," said Jenkins, "is the switch that diverts the trains onto this maintenance track."

He pointed to a clear plastic box on the wall with a big red button behind it.

"You press that button, and that curved track out there pushes inward, while a straight piece of track swings in to fill the gap. Then the trains are diverted in here."

Habst nodded.

"And you can't do that while the ride is running, because they'll come onto this track too fast and will get damaged when they hit the barrier at the end. So when that big red button is pressed, the whole ride stops, and you gotta push the trains by hand."

"Wow," said Habst.

"And!" said Jenkins, "You can't just move one damned car in here! Those four cars are linked together with heavy steel beams. No way to separate them without moving all four cars in here and unlinking them. If you want to service anything other than the first car, you have to unlink them, back all four out, flip the switch, separate them on the main track, flip the switch again, push in the broken one, flip the switch again, back up the ones that were in front of the broken one on the main track, flip the switch again, pull the other three back into here, link them together, back them up, flip the switch again, and let those move away on the main track."

"That's nuts."

"Exactly. So you see the issue? It'd take an hour, minimum, to get a single car back here. And you'd have to do a ride shutdown before that happens, so add another half hour to clear out the queue, stop everything, and then start it all again afterward."

"So...."

"So if you're gonna do a goddamned ride shutdown during the day, then you might as well just do a 101 to clean the damned car! The only time we need to be pulling a single car back here is when it has physical damage. And even then, considering the low attendance we get, we're better off just pulling the whole string of four back and saying 'fuck it' to splitting one car off!"

Habst nodded in agreement.

"Okay, you understand now? Good. Then get the hell out of here, show those idiots in Ride Ops your video, and tell them to read a goddamned operations guide before they make any more ignorant requests of Jenkins!"

"Yes, sir!"

"I like you, son. You ever want to move over to Maintenance, you let me know. They'll be forcing me out soon – mandatory retirement – so someone will need to take over this mess."

"I might just take you up on that, Jenkins," said Habst, without a hint of sarcasm.

They shook hands and Habst walked out of the maintenance bay. He turned the camera to his face.

"That dude is cool. Please don't screw with him."

He uploaded the video to YouTube.

And that was it. His mission was complete.

But now his real mission began. Find Sat-Com, determine

if he was a threat, and take him down if necessary.

He walked across the road and stepped into the wooded area behind the Canada pavilion. He had a clear view of the entrance to the maintenance bay.

Habst sat down, and waited.

And waited.

And waited.

He smoked a bowl.

And waited.

# TWENTY-FIVE

*The following document was declassified in 2007, per a Freedom of Information Act request:*

CENTRAL INTELLIGENCE AGENCY

Intelligence Information Cable

WARNING NOTICE

SENSITIVE INTELLIGENCE SOURCES AND
METHODS INVOLVED
NOT RELEASABLE TO FOREIGN NATIONALS
NOT RELEASABLE TO CONTRACTORS OR
CONTRACTOR/CONSULTANTS.

REPORT CLASS: SECRET

DOI: LATE APRIL 1982 - 05 JANUARY 1983

SUBJECT: Asset debriefing re Agent
CG 8094-S and WED-Com computing
technologies.

With respect to the attached, it is suggested that this report be transmitted by Top Secret letter to Mr. Lexington for the information of the President, to the Vice President, to the Under-Secretary of the State Department, to the Attorney General, and to Director Webster of the FBI.

BACKGROUND:

Private contractor WED-Com runs a nuclear reactor outside of Provo, Utah. This is common knowledge within the Agency. The reactor has been operating safely for nearly twenty years, and in that time WED-Com has fully cooperated with the Agency in assuring the safety and security of the reactor and the fissile material contained therein. Since the company is a longtime military contractor, they have been granted full permission to continue to run the nuclear reactor, as long as it is deemed necessary for military-related projects and/or research.

As part of our goal of increasing the security of fissile material, the Agency decided to send Agent CG 8094-S into the WED-Com site for a period of six months. During this time, the agent was deep undercover, posing as an installation technician for the generator's new cooling structure. The agent conducted

wide surveillance of not only the nuclear
activities of WED-Com, but also of other
key functions of the organization.

DETAILS:

Agent CG 8094-S arrived on the site on
26 APRIL 1982 and immediately began work
on the upgrade of the central cooling
tower for the site's nuclear reactor.
During his introductory briefing, Agent
CG 8094-S asked the project supervisor
why the upgrade was being performed.
The supervisor claimed that the site's
power requirements had increased
exponentially over the past year alone,
and the tower upgrade was needed to more
efficiently cool the reactor. When asked
why power consumption had increased
so dramatically, the supervisor seemed
unclear as to the answer, only knowing
that it had something to do with newer,
faster computers in the datacenter.
With this in mind, on 9 MAY 1982,
Agent CG 8094-S was able to gain access
to the datacenter by volunteering to
perform emergency maintenance on the
datacenter's air conditioning system,
a task for which he was qualified, but
not authorized, to perform. However,
it was Mother's Day and the normal air
conditioning repair staff were not on-
site and could not be contacted. Agent
CG 8094-S, who was working that day,
overheard the datacenter's maintenance

supervisor making a phone call to an off-site staff member, requesting that the staff member drive to the site and perform the maintenance. The call ended with the supervisor yelling and banging the phone receiver against the wall, at which point Agent CG 8094-S volunteered his help, and was promptly escorted into the datacenter.

While Agent CG 8094-S is not an expert in computer technology, he had received the standard Agency training in cybersecurity and had been in multiple datacenters during his civilian career as a cooling systems technician. As a result, he was able to describe what he saw in the datacenter in great detail, although it is the opinion of the Agency that his observations were deeply flawed.

From Agent CG 8094-S's written report:
"I was blindfolded and driven via some sort of motorized vehicle deep underground. After approximately thirty minutes we reached our destination, my blindfold was removed, and I was granted access to a room the size of two football fields. I was told this was the datacenter, although I did not observe any standard mainframes inside the room. There were many standard-sized mainframe cabinets, but they did not contain any magnetic media or tube-based machinery. The cabinets were arranged in rows of thirty, and there were approximately

three hundred rows. Each row of thirty was subdivided into ten three-cabinet groups. The first of the three in each group was filled with dozens of small machines, approximately two inches high, which stretched the width and depth of each cabinet. The second cabinet contained much larger flat panels in the center, surrounded on the top and bottom by hundreds of approximately four-inch vertical slots, all of which had a single rapidly blinking green light at their edge. The third contained what seemed to be the communications hub for the other two cabinets, with hundreds of color-coded cables running from the other two cabinets into the top of it, which were then fanned out and attached to strips of plugs on the front. There was also another large bundle of cables coming out of the top of the cabinet and running out of the datacenter. None of the cables appeared to be standard copper cabling, but were instead millimeters thick with dual plastic connectors.

"I also noticed quickly that the cooling system was quite advanced. All of the machines were air cooled, and the noise in the datacenter was extremely loud as a result. Each row of cabinets alternated front/back placement so that the rear of two adjacent rows pointed to a center aisle that was designated a 'hot aisle'. Above the hot aisle was an air conditioner intake vent which removed the hot air blown from the rear of each cabinet. The front of each cabinet faced a 'cool aisle' which contained floor-mounted air conditioner output ducts. Each hot and cold aisle was separated by what appeared to be Plexiglas attached to the top of each row of cabinets."

We showed Agent CG 8094-S's report on the datacenter to multiple Agency computer engineers, datacenter architects, and hardware designers. While they all understood the hot/cool aisle concept and commended the layout's ingenuity and efficiency, none were able to identify any of the equipment Agent CG 8094-S described. One expert called it "pure nonsense" while another claimed that Agent CG 8094-S had "seen too many science-fiction movies".

However, it was Agent CG 8094-S's description of events from 30 SEPTEMBER 1982, in what he called a "War Room", which must lead us to believe he is either compromised or mentally unstable.

From Agent CG 8094-S's debriefing interview:

"WED-Com was going to drastically increase power production and consumption for a new project, and wanted a cooling engineer on-site in case the temperature began to rise or fluctuate beyond specifications. I volunteered, and once again I was blindfolded and driven underground, this time into what appeared to be a War Room. There were huge television screens on the walls displaying all types of graphics. The television screens were thin and flat, much like a movie screen, but I couldn't see any projector units on the ceilings or walls, and people walking in front of the screens didn't block out the image. I looked around the rear of one of the walls where a particularly large screen was mounted, and found it to be mounted to a foot of solid concrete. On the other side of the concrete another screen was mounted, ruling out rear projection as the source of the images.

"I was placed in front of a screen displaying graphs and numerical readouts of the ambient temperature of each row of cabinets in the datacenter, as well as readouts from multiple sensors in the reactor. From my position, I could see the operations of nearly the entire War Room.

"At approximately thirteen hundred hours, a male voice broadcast a message to the War Room over an intercom. The voice said, 'Roger, commence boot sequence,' and a few seconds later another male voice, presumably Roger, said, 'Boot sequence initiated.' I immediately noticed a sizeable spike in the ambient temperature in the datacenter, as well as a smaller increase in the reactor temperature. The temperature in the datacenter remained rather high, but leveled out at around one hundred degrees Fahrenheit, while the reactor temperature almost immediately returned to normal. I was pleased by this, because it meant that the upgrades we'd done on the cooling tower had been successful. A few people cheered.

"Almost fifteen minutes later, Roger stated, 'Boot sequence completed,' and there was another round of cheers. The first male voice, who I was finally able to identify as coming from an older gray-haired man at the front of the room, then said, 'Enable speech subprogram,' which was quickly followed by Roger ack'ing the command.

"A few seconds later, Roger said 'Speech subprogram activated,' and a low, raspy groan filled the room, emanating from speakers all around us.

"It sent shivers down my spine.

"The groan went on and on, unbroken by a breath.

"The older man then said, 'Activate auditory input subprogram,' and Roger gave the ack. But before he could say it was activated, the groan turned into a horrible, pain-filled, piercing scream, and everyone in the room put their hands up to their ears.

"'Reduce auditory input gain by eighty dBs!' yelled the older man. Roger didn't bother sending an ack; he just did it. Within seconds, the screaming stopped, and returned back to a slightly higher-pitched and shaky groan.

"I could hear the old man yell, 'Jesus fucking Christ,' from across the room, although that didn't go out over the intercom. I watched him wipe his face with his hand, and then he took a deep breath and pressed the intercom button.

"He said, 'Walt, it's Card. Can you hear me?'

"Right after he said that, the low groan switched to distorted alien-like gibberish, and it kept going for at least twenty minutes. It reminded me of the interrogation resistance training we agents have to go through. I could barely stand it, to be honest. At least a dozen people got up and ran out of the room, sobbing. The old man, Card, looked over at a screen next to him, read something on there, and said into his microphone, 'You can't use your mouth right now, Walt. Just concentrate very hard on thinking the words out loud.' He turned off the intercom and yelled, 'Don't shut it down! We gotta get this vocal interface tested and debugged.'

"Then slowly the gibberish started turning into actual words. I could make out 'blind', 'paralyzed', and 'accident'. Card said, 'Roger, modify the subprogram on the fly. Slowly increase the filtering bandwidth to get rid of the noise'. Roger gave an ack, then said, 'Filter modified.'

"And then the voice started speaking in sentences.

"It said, 'Card, I'm blind and paralyzed, and everything sounds strange. Was I in an accident?'

"Card said, 'Something like that. Hold on a second and we'll get your sight fixed.' He said over the intercom, 'Activate visual input subprogram.' He got an ack and a 'Visual input subprogram activated.'

"The voice said, 'I can see now. It's very… sharp. Too much detail. And why am I on the ceiling?'

"Everyone in the room looked up at the ceiling, I guess expecting to see someone strapped up there. Card looked up and waved, and I noticed that he was waving straight at a videocamera mounted on the wall at the front of the room.

"The voice said, 'You look awful, Card. And is that Joe, Roger, and Wathel I see over there? Hi, boys. You all look awful, too.' Some other people in the room chuckled and waved at the camera, and I felt the mood lighten significantly.

"Card then said, 'Initial sensory tests successful. Congratulations, everyone.' There was a lot of cheering and clapping. Then he said, 'Thank you all for your help. Now please clear the room so I can start the debriefing.'

"And that was it. Everyone cleared the room, aside from Card and three other men, who I'm assuming were Joe, Roger, and Wathel. I was blindfolded and brought back to the surface, and the next day my WED-Com contract was terminated and my access was revoked."

When Agent CG 8094-S was asked what he thought had happened at WED-Com that day, his response was as follows:

"I think they brought somebody back to life in a computer. Somebody they all knew. Somebody important. And he's in there now. In those rows and rows of machines in that datacenter. Alive."

After this debriefing Agent CG 8094-S requested a leave of absence from the Agency due to mental stress, which was granted.

CONCLUSION:

While Agent CG 8094-S's account is certainly captivating, it also seems completely unbelievable and is possibly the result of psychotic hallucinations. However, as the Agency is not satisfied with leaving loose ends dangling, we sent Agent 7993-S into the facility under deep cover in early NOVEMBER 1982. Agent 7993-S is one of our most experienced recon experts.

Over the course of three months in the facility, he could find no access points leading to any underground utilities or work areas. He did not observe a single instance of any staff member riding any sort of motorized vehicle within the facility. And, after covertly acquiring full clearance to access every door in the facility, he found no evidence of a War Room or massive datacenter. He found only a typical server room filled with standard mainframes and input terminals. Finally, he was not able to verify that any employees named "Card" or "Wathel" worked at the facility.

Our recommendation is that this case be closed, and that Agent 8094-S be terminated from the Agency. Considering his mental instability, it is suggested that he is a high-level security risk, and that he be placed under constant Agency-supervised psychiatric care and not be allowed to communicate with the outside world.

In summary, while the information herein is interesting, Agent CG 8094-S's account is unreliable. As a result, I do not believe it is sufficiently startling to justify a briefing of the President.

REPORT CLASS: SECRET

WARNING NOTICE

SENSITIVE INTELLIGENCE SOURCES AND METHODS INVOLVED
NOT RELEASABLE TO FOREIGN NATIONALS
NOT RELEASABLE TO CONTRACTORS OR CONTRACTOR/CONSULTANTS.

# TWENTY-SIX

NIGHT FELL, AND HABST was in the sixth hour of his stakeout. Given the nature of what he'd shot earlier in the day, he didn't expect Sat-Com to show up while the park was still operating.

His phone had been ringing constantly. Charlie wouldn't stop calling. At first he'd left threatening messages, which had turned to pleading messages, which had turned back to threatening, and then to a simple "Call me".

He felt bad about how he'd treated Charlie, but letting him in on the plan just wasn't worth the risk. He had to do this by himself, per Sat-Com's instructions, and hope for the best.

An hour after Charlie's last call, he received a text message from Monika's number.

*We need to talk. Please let me know where you are.*

*I would love to talk things out,* wrote Habst. *I'm really sorry about what happened. But I'm sure your hand is killing you. I'll come to you.*

*No, I'm much better now. Would like to get out of the house. Where are you?*

*Is Charlie there with you?*

No response.

*That's what I thought. Nice try. I love you.*

He turned off the phone and sat silently for a few minutes. He pulled his vaporizer from his backpack, took a few hits, and then sat for a few minutes longer. Needing another distraction, he retrieved the night-vision goggles from the bag, put them on, and powered them up. And sure enough, he could see into the dark woods around him as clear as day.

"Cool," he said.

He looked up at the sky just as fireworks exploded over World Showcase Lagoon. It was the grand finale of *IllumiNations*.

"Aarrrghhh!" yelled Habst as the goggles amplified the explosion into a blinding white burst of light. He yanked off the goggles and threw them on the ground.

"Goddamned technology!" he said, temporarily blinded.

A few minutes later his eyesight was just about back to normal. He squinted in pain and shielded his eyes as fireworks lit up the sky with the intensity of the noon sun. Seconds after the finale ended, he heard the roar of thousands of Guests rushing to the front gate.

Finally, the park would be empty, and it would be time for Sat-Com to make his appearance.

But by 2AM Habst was sick of waiting.

"What is taking that bastard so long?"

He stood up, stretched, walked down from the hill, and headed back towards the interior of the park.

The walkways backstage were actually more crowded at night than during the day. His Custodial uniform ensured that he remained pretty much invisible to the other Cast Members, but it was still unnerving to see so many people walking around. He could only assume that Charlie Walker had the entirety of the Walt Disney World security team scouring the parks, looking for him.

Crossing through the switchback from backstage to the Imagination pavilion, he poked his head out into the park, saw it lit with floodlights, and decided that leaving his stakeout spot probably hadn't been the best idea. Better to go back and deal with the boredom.

He heard a familiar whirring noise, and looked up.

The monorail with the *Duffy: The Movie* wrap glided along the track in front of the Imagination pavilion.

*That's weird*, thought Habst. *Why in the hell is the monorail running this late?*

Without drawing attention to himself he walked as quickly as he could towards the monorail station at the front entrance.

Out of breath, he arrived at the turnstiles just in time to see two men step out of the cockpit of the Duffyrail. The station was dark, and he could only see their silhouettes. Both men were tall and lanky. They both carried duffel bags. One man put his arm around the other's shoulder, and they both laughed, sauntering down the ramp in a completely relaxed, casual, and confident manner.

Very strange. They acted like they belonged there. Like they owned the place. Were they executives? They had that swagger. But what would two executives be doing in the park in the middle of the night?

Habst had a hunch that one of these men was Sat-Com. Or maybe they both were. Hell, Sat-Com could be a whole group of people for all he knew. An army of saboteurs and terrorists like Al Qaeda, plotting to destroy theme parks all around the world. But why? To what end? What was the point?

He knew these questions wouldn't be answered until he caught Sat-Com. So he decided to follow the men. If they went to the locations in the videos, he'd know that one or both of them were the saboteurs.

And then?

And then he'd catch them and grill them, and if they seemed like a threat, he'd bring them to Bill Ivers. Somehow. He hadn't planned on taking down two guys. One he could handle, but two would be much more difficult. He was in good shape, but it wasn't like he was a kung fu expert or anything.

And his shoulder still hurt. He should have stolen one of Charlie's taser guns. Instead, he'd just have to hit them with something heavy.

Habst squatted behind a planter as the men walked to the front gate, jumped the turnstiles with an easy grace, and walked up to one of the Leave a Legacy rocks.

That's when Habst got his first good look at them.

They were young, in their twenties, and looked like they might be brothers. Both had straight dark hair, long in the front, which they kept brushing back whenever it fell over their foreheads. The taller man had a long, jowly face. The shorter man had a similar face, and sported a thin moustache, which was immaculately groomed.

The shorter man turned his head out of the shadows and towards Habst, and Habst realized with a start that this was the same person who had saved Monika's life in the *Carousel of Progress*.

And now, seeing his face straight-on, Habst had no doubt.

It was Walt Disney.

Habst fell backward, shocked.

Impossible.

Utterly impossible.

But yet, there he was, as clear as day. A spitting image of the world-famous entrepreneur Habst had seen in so many documentaries and books. One of the most recognizable men in modern history was standing no less than thirty feet from him.

And with this recognition came a realization that the other man was none other than Roy Disney, Walt's brother. While Roy had tended to stay out of the spotlight, Habst had seen plenty of pictures of him, and there was no mistaking Walt's brother's unique and world-weary face.

These were obviously highly sophisticated disguises, Habst decided. *Mission: Impossible*-level shit. Because there was no way that two men who had been dead for over forty years were walking around Epcot as twenty-something versions of themselves. These were doppelgängers, and part of their plan somehow involved them looking like the founders of the Walt Disney Company. Habst couldn't imagine why any plan would require such a ruse, but he figured he'd find out once he caught the bastards.

Habst watched in amazement as the two men, in rapid, coordinated movements, pulled spools of wire from their duffel bags and began winding it around the base of each granite block. At the center of each block they stuck a large piece of white stuff resembling silly putty onto the wire. Habst had seen enough movies to know that these white things were C-4 plastic explosives.

The men moved like ballet dancers as they went about their task. Habst sat captivated as they floated between the tombstones with a contagious youthful exuberance. He couldn't help but smile.

He continued to stare in wonderment as the men finished their task, linked arms, and skipped towards Future World East.

Towards Mission: SPACE.

When they were out of visual range, Habst walked out from behind the planter and squatted down in front of one of the tombstones. He looked at the wire, touched the white sticky blob stuck to it, brought his finger up to his nose, and sniffed. He realized that he had no idea what C-4 smelled like. He then realized that if it was C-4, it could go off at any time and blow him to smithereens. He jumped back, and ran after the brothers.

He saw them just as they were entering the ride building. Deciding there was no good reason to follow them in, he held back, waiting behind a head-high concrete landscaping structure near the pavilion.

Sure enough, ten minutes later, the two men exited the ride and sauntered past him towards the large corridor between

Mouse Gear and Electric Umbrella.

"Having a good time yet, Roy?" asked the shorter man, slapping the taller man on the back.

"I'll be happy when it's finally over," said Roy.

"Christ! Just enjoy the moment, why donchya? It's exciting, like something right out of one of those live-action adventures we used to make. Hell, you even look a bit like Kirk Douglas, you know that?"

Roy laughed.

"You know damn well that's not true, Walt," he said. "You and I both know that I look a lot more like Goofy than I do Kirk."

Walt let out a big toothy guffaw, and slapped Roy on the back again.

"Holy shit," said Habst.

These guys must be delusional. That was it. They were mentally insane. They actually thought they were Walt and Roy. Just like those crazy Vegas impersonators who played their characters for so long that they begin to think they *were* Marilyn Monroe or Elvis or whoever. Except those people didn't go around blowing things up. At least not that he was aware of, anyway.

As expected, the two men walked backstage behind Imagination. Habst followed them to the maintenance bay, where they disappeared into darkness.

Habst pulled Charlie's night-vision goggles out of his bag, put them on, and powered them up. He could clearly see Walt and Roy doing something to the big red track button on the wall. Roy held a voltmeter while Walt cut a wire leading to the button, stripped the ends with a pocketknife, pulled a small circuit board from his duffel bag, and clipped the two bare wires to either end of it. He looked at Roy, who looked at the voltmeter and nodded.

Habst ducked behind the contraption used to clean the 3D glasses as the brothers walked within two feet of him.

"We're done here," said Roy. "Make the call."

Walt pulled a cell phone from his pocket and dialed a number.

"I'd like to report a bomb in Epcot.

"That's right. A bomb.

"Well, I'd say you might want to evacuate the place, don't you think?"

Walt hung up the phone.

"Time to get out of here?" said Roy.

"Yep. Race ya!" said Walt.

"No way."

"Well, I'm runnin'. And I know you don't want me to leave you here."

"You wouldn't."

Walt grinned and took off running. He ran so fast that Habst literally saw a blur though the night-vision goggles as Walt zoomed out of the building. Habst had never seen anyone run that fast before. He pulled off the goggles in disbelief.

"Dammit, Walt!" yelled Roy. He took off after his brother, running just as fast.

"Shit," said Habst. He threw the goggles in his bag and ran after the men.

He saw them turn the corner around the building, heading back into the park. But when he finally made it onstage, the men had vanished, and there was a crowd of Cast Members running directly towards him.

He started pushing through the crowd, trying to look over them for the two brothers.

"You're going the wrong way!" yelled a manager as Habst pushed past him. "We're evacuating!"

"I left my broom in The Land!" yelled Habst.

"What?!"

"I gotta get my broom! And my dustpan!"

The manager started to say something else but was pushed along with the tide of people rushing to the back gate of the park.

Once he'd broken through the crowd, Habst stopped, looked around, and saw no sign of the men.

He thought for a second, remembered the monorail video that he'd shot, and ran to the station.

Sure enough, he reached the station just in time to see the two men board the front of the monorail.

"Dammit!" he said, running as fast as he could up to the loading platform.

The monorail started to pull away as Habst reached the platform.

Without thinking, he ran to the end of the station, scaled the metal guard rail, and jumped onto the roof of the second car of the monorail.

He steadied himself as the monorail cleared the station and picked up speed. Holding tightly onto the handrail on the roof of the train, he crawled carefully towards the pilot's cab.

---

In the pilot's cab, Walt and Roy looked at each other intently. Walt held the same Android HTC that Habst owned.

"Do it," said Roy.

Walt tapped the screen.

Back in the park, three things happened simultaneously:

In Imagination, the track switch was activated. The small piece of curved track pivoted out of the way, as the straight piece next to it joined with the track that led to the maintenance bay. Then, the ride came to life, and the cars started moving.

The brothers had disabled the track switch's failsafe.

Within seconds, moving trains started heading into the maintenance bay. The first one slammed against the steel barrier at the end of the track, cracking its chassis. The next train rear-ended the first one, cracking its chassis even more, and causing a door to fall off. As each subsequent set of cars zoomed into the bay, the force on the front train increased, until the barrier at the end finally snapped and the train flew six feet across the maintenance bay and slammed to the ground, shattering the fiberglass chassis, and crushing the frame. Every train in the ride soon met a similar fate, until the bay was filled with mangled ride vehicles, all destroyed beyond repair.

Across the park, in the Mission: SPACE simulator bays, the centrifuges whirred to life. As they picked up speed, the individual pods began to vibrate violently. Each high-load linkage that tied the pods to the large spinning arms had been weakened by the brothers with a surgical cut from an oxyfuel torch. When the centrifuges reached their maximum speed, each pod tore off its arm, moving at a few hundred miles per hour.

Two of the pods hit the ground, shattered the concrete floor, bounced straight up in the air, and tore through the roof of the building. One landed a half mile away in the empty parking lot, while the other crashed through Duffy's meet-and-greet gazebo, obliterating it.

The rest of the pods ripped through the walls of the building like buckshot tearing through flesh, completely destroying everything in their path.

Seconds later, with all structural supports demolished, the building imploded.

Finally, at the front of the park, the C-4 explosives detonated in a huge flash. When the dust cleared moments later, the Leave a Legacy tombstones had vanished, reduced to rubble.

---

THE SHOCKWAVE FROM the Leave a Legacy blast hit the monorail just as Habst reached the pilot's cab. The train shuddered, and Habst was thrown forward from the top of the monorail onto the window of the cockpit.

"Ahhh shiiiiit!" yelled Habst.

He grabbed the flashing light at the top of the cab, but his grip was tenuous at best. The residual rumbling from the bombs combined with the normal jitter of the poorly maintained track caused him to repeatedly slam into the cockpit window, crotch first.

"Christ!" yelled Walt from inside the cockpit.

"Holy cow!" said Roy.

"Help! I'm losing my grip!" yelled Habst, his face pressed against the window, a mere three feet from Walt.

"Hold on!" yelled Walt. He turned to Roy. "I don't want to stop this thing. We can't risk a delay. Can you get out there and help that idiot?"

"Sure thing," said Roy.

Roy unlocked the escape hatch on the ceiling of the cockpit, flung it open, and pulled himself to the roof of the speeding vehicle. He stood up, steady as a rock, walked two steps to the window, grabbed Habst's arms, and pulled him up with the grace of an acrobat. Still holding onto Habst, Roy pivoted and dropped him through the escape hatch into the cockpit.

"Oof," said Habst, as he smashed into the curved passenger seat and tumbled to the floor.

Roy looked down and jumped feet-first through the hatch. He stuck the landing perfectly, and pulled Habst to his feet.

"You almost got yourself killed!" yelled Walt.

"What the hell do you think you're doing?!" asked Roy.

"I'm trying to catch you two," said Habst, breathing heavily, "so I can save Charlie's job and keep myself out of prison."

"Jesus Christ!" said Walt. "We told you not to worry about any of that. Why couldn't you just trust us?"

"Trust you?! Are you kidding me? You assholes set me up! I'm an accessory to like eighty million crimes now!"

"We always intended to deal with that," said Walt. "Like we said, as long as you did your part, we'd do our part. Once this night is over, everything will be fine."

"Exactly," said Roy. "Who do you think posted your million dollar bail?"

"You guys did that?"

"Who the hell else would have paid a million dollars to get you out of jail?" asked Walt.

"That's a lot of money!" said Roy.

"Everything is going to be fine," said Walt. "Insurance will pay for all of the damage, and everything will be rebuilt bigger and better. We'll make sure Charlie doesn't lose his job. And you'll be a free man. A rich one, too."

"Rich?"

"Really rich," said Roy.

"I can dig that," said Habst. He sized up the men. "So, wait. Are you both Sat-Com? And are you really Walt and Roy Disney?"

"Yes," said Roy.

"And, yes," said Walt.

"Holy shit," said Habst. "I have no idea what's going on."

"It'll make more sense in a few days," said Walt. "All you need to know now is that Roy and I are alive and well, and if all goes as planned, things are going to be a lot better.... For everyone, everywhere."

"That sounds pretty intense."

"My brother has a flair for dramatic pitches," said Roy, smiling at Walt.

"This is insane. I don't understand how you're alive," said Habst.

"It's... complicated," said Walt.

"Uh, yeah," said Habst. "You've both been dead for decades. It better be really complicated!"

Walt and Roy laughed.

"Show him," said Walt, nodding to Roy.

Roy lifted his shirt. Underneath was heavy-duty black fabric.

"Bullet and knife proof," said Walt.

Roy yanked at a tab on the fabric near his ribs. It made a distinctive noise.

"I'm a big fan of Velcro," said Walt. "One of the best inventions ever."

Pulling the tab made a large section of the bulletproof fabric tear away, revealing the interior of Roy's torso. Inside was a mostly empty area, aside from a thin metallic framework, and a blue-tinted transparent tube where his spine should have been. The tube was filled with tightly packed wiring.

"Whoa!" said Habst, stumbling back a few steps.

"Everything is fiber optics and miniature actuators now," said Walt. "Wish we'd had those damned things when we were building Lincoln. They save so much space and are infinitely more precise than hydraulics or pneumatics."

"Uh… what?" asked Habst.

Roy closed up his torso.

"We're animatronics," he said.

"Huh?"

"Robots. We're robots."

"I know what animatronics are," said Habst, regaining his footing. "I just don't understand how there are two standing in front of me, moving around of their own volition."

Habst poked at Roy's torso. Roy poked him back.

"Our brains, if you want to call them that, are in a datacenter a few miles from here," said Walt. "We're controlling the animatronics through a custom-built wi-fi setup. Got our own satellite in a geostationary orbit directly above us!"

"So that's what Sat-Com stands for," said Habst. "Satellite Communications."

"Nope," said Walt, "but good guess. Not going to spill the beans on that one yet. You'll find out soon enough."

"So… you're animatronics who think you're Walt and Roy Disney. The fact that I'm even remotely buying this freaks me out."

"We don't think we're Walt and Roy Disney," said Walt.

"We are Walt and Roy Disney."

"That's not possible," said Habst.

"Neither are free-roaming animatronics," said Roy. "Look, none of this is possible with known technology. Luckily, we're not limited to working with known technology."

"We're Walt and Roy because we've had every neuron of our brains digitally modelled," said Walt. "Every single one. The high-res imaging of my brain alone took four years to complete. Took another twelve years to create the model. Couldn't get us out into the real world until a few years ago, though. We were confined to the datacenter. To the inside of the servers. You'd think it'd be boring, but it was pretty goddamned exciting, to be honest. Built a whole world in there over the past thirty years."

"So your head really was frozen?"

"No," said Walt. "Back in the sixties, even the best cryogenic technology produced microscopic ice crystals which severely damaged neural cells. My boys came up with a much better technique for preserving that specific type of tissue. Or, at least the best technique for our intended endgame."

"Wow."

"Best investment we ever made," said Roy.

"And now you're back, and are destroying the parks like some goddamned Terminators. Wonderful. Hooray for technology."

"We're not destroying the…," Walt trailed off, looking out the window. "That was the marker, Roy."

"What's going on?" asked Habst.

"This is it," said Walt.

"Okay," said Roy.

"Uh…," said Habst.

"Are the safeties disabled?" asked Walt.

Roy looked down at his phone.

"Confirmed."

Walt slammed the gear knob to the highest setting, and

the monorail doubled its speed in a matter of seconds.

Habst braced himself.

"What the hell, guys?!"

"Bill Ivers cares more about turning these damned things into moving billboards than he does about the safety of the Cast Members and the Guests," said Walt. "The transportation of the future does not kill twenty-one-year-old boys."

"So you're destroying it? C'mon! Once again, I am definitely in the wrong place at the wrong time."

"Gotta move now!" said Roy. "What are we going to do with him?"

"I'll hold him," said Walt.

"Wait, what?!" said Habst.

Roy opened the passenger door, nodded at Walt, and jumped out.

"Oh shit!" yelled Habst, leaning out the door and watching Roy fall out of sight into the blackness below.

Walt grabbed Habst around his waist.

"Relax your muscles. You don't want any tension when we hit the ground."

"Wait, wait, wait!"

"Here we go!"

Walt jumped, dragging a screaming Habst with him.

Habst promptly shit his pants.

Walt rotated expertly in midair, pulling Habst close. He curled them both into a loose ball, and hit the ground rolling. The speed of their rotation caused Habst to fly out of Walt's grasp and continue to roll another forty feet through the grass until he finally smashed into a patch of palm fronds and landed in a muddy ditch.

Behind him, the monorail, traveling at least sixty miles an hour, reached the sharp curve that turned into the darkened Ticket and Transportation Center.

Sparks flew as the front car tilted onto its side, not able to properly bank the turn at that speed. Its wheels separated from the beam and it jumped the track, taking the rest of the train with it.

As it soared through the air it smashed through the Resort Loop and the Magic Kingdom tracks, which ran parallel to the Epcot track on that particular curve. Both tracks disintegrated, their support beams tumbling like dominos for a hundred meters in both directions.

Before fully leaving the beam, the two rear cars of the train snapped like a whip, cracking the Epcot track in half, smashing one of the support beams, and sending tons of concrete crashing to the ground.

Completely free of its track, for a moment the monorail floated through space, looking like a jet without wings. This glorious sight only lasted a few seconds before it landed on the grass next to the TTC with an incredible crash. Still moving at a rapid pace, it dug an eighty-foot trench into the tundra and finally ground to a halt.

The Duffyrail was destroyed past all hope of repair, mangled and on fire, debris scattered across three acres of land. The track, too, was later determined to be so structurally damaged that at least a mile of each line coming out of the TTC would need to be demolished and rebuilt to ensure any sort of stability.

Habst turned his head away from the destruction to find Walt and Roy standing over him.

"You did it," whispered Habst.

"We did it," said Walt. "Thank you. You passed the test. You won."

Roy slowly looked Habst up and down, his eyes glowing bright blue.

"He's fine. A few broken bones and a collapsed lung. But he's fine. He'll be alright."

"We'll be in touch," said Walt. "Shouldn't be more than a week or so. Keep your laptop and phone with you. You're gonna love what happens next."

Circular beams of light flickered across the woods next to them.

"Time to go!" said Roy.

"See ya, friend," said Walt.

They both ran off at nearly supersonic speeds as the flashlight beams grew closer.

In too much pain to move, Habst laid his head down on the soft mud, stared up at the stars and waited to be found.

"Well, at least I'm not constipated anymore," he said.

# TWENTY-SEVEN

HABST AWOKE IN a hospital bed. Disoriented, he tried to sit, but stopped when the pain in his chest reminded him that he was there for a reason. He'd broken his left femur, right collarbone, three ribs, right wrist and every finger on that hand, and had collapsed his right lung.

Charlie Walker ambled up to the bed.

He looked pissed.

"You're a real son of a bitch, you know that?"

"Everything will be fine, Charlie. They promised, and I trust them. Now you'll have to trust me."

"Trust you?! After you ransacked my house, sent me on an all-night wild goose chase, and were a co-conspirator in a criminal plot that caused millions, if not billions, of dollars of damage to the parks I've been charged to protect?!"

"I'm sorry. I did what I did because it was the only way I could fix all the shit I'd messed up. I went behind your back because I knew you wouldn't ever in a million years go along with it. But everything is going to be okay. I don't know what else to tell you, man. I really believe everything will work out fine."

"I know it will, Habst," said Charlie, breaking into a broad grin. "All of your charges have been dropped. I already got my raise. The insurance company is running a full investigation of the sabotage incidents, but there's been surprisingly little press about it. I don't know how you did it, but you actually came through this time, you crazy idiot. You actually did something right for once!"

"Really?!"

"Really."

"Wow, that's awesome, man!"

Habst looked around.

"Wait. How long have I been out?"

"A few days. Not too bad considering you went through a half-dozen different surgeries. Can't believe you fell from a speeding monorail with only a few broken bones and a collapsed lung. You're a lucky bastard."

"It wasn't luck. Walt saved me."

"Uh huh. Again with the Walt stuff?"

"I'm serious. Walt really did save me. And he told me… crap. Are my laptop and phone here?"

"Sure. I figured you'd want them at some point. Probably to buy more pot, but at this point, who am I to judge? Seems like you have a free pass from the legal system to do whatever you want."

Charlie handed the laptop and phone to Habst.

Habst unlocked the phone and saw that he had a new text message.

*Roy here. Check your HackNCrackBB inbox. Set you up with a brokerage account. Also, Friday, 4:30PM EDT. We're doing a press conference. Should be on most of the major news stations. Be sure to tune in. Hope you're recovering quickly. Walt sends his best.*

"Charlie, what day is it?"

"Friday."

"Damn. What time is it?"

"A little after four PM."

"Oh good, we haven't missed it. Can you turn on the TV to CNN or something?"

"Sure. What's up?"

"Sat-Com says they're doing a press conference."

"Sat-Com is doing a press conference? This should be interesting."

Habst cracked open his XFR laptop, started Tor, and logged into his HackNCrackBB account. A message was waiting in his inbox from Sat-Com, with a link to ShareBuilder.com, a username, a password, and the following:

*Used your 1K VTC to buy these shares. DO NOT SELL THEM BEFORE 4:30PM EDT ON FRIDAY!*

"Oh, c'mon!" said Habst.

He logged into ShareBuilder and saw he now owned about sixty-five thousand shares of Sat-Com, Inc. They were worth $2 each.

"Total bullshit."

"What's going on?" asked Charlie.

"Those jerks promised me one thousand virtcoins and gave me some stock instead. I can't buy pot with this crap."

He hit the trade button, entered 65,000 as the number of shares he wanted to sell, set it as a market order, and pressed sell.

After ten minutes, nobody had filled a single share of the order.

"Dammit," said Habst. "I'm never going to unload this shit."

A minute later, he received a text message.

*I SAID DON'T SELL, YOU FOOL! CANCEL THE TRADE! THE PRESS CONFERENCE STARTS IN A FEW MINUTES!*

"Christ, fine," said Habst, canceling the sale and looking up at Charlie. "You wanna buy some stock? Great company. The owners are computer simulations of long-dead theme park moguls. Oh, what's that? You think I'm insane? You'd never put a dime into such a company?"

Habst threw his laptop across the room.

"Well, neither would I, because it makes no goddamned sense! Freakin' hucksters took me for a ride!"

"But hey, at least you're not going to rot in jail for the rest of your life, right?" said a soft voice from the doorway.

"Monika?!"

"Well, I'll be damned," said Charlie.

Monika walked up to the bed and brushed Habst's cheek with her undamaged left hand.

"Oh man, it is so great to see you," said Habst.

"Good to see you, too, Habst. How are you feeling? Concussion? Spinal damage?"

"Nope, just some broken bones."

"Oh, good," said Monika. "Then I won't feel so bad about this."

She pulled back her arm and socked him straight in the eye with an expertly thrown left hook.

"Ah, goddammit!" said Habst, shielding his face.

"That's for bankrupting us and making us lose the house! Now we have to move into a goddamned condo in a second-rate golf resort in… ugh… Winter Park."

She shuddered, turned, raised her closed fist over her head, and slammed it down onto Habst's crotch.

"Ahhhhhhhhh!!!"

"And that's for fucking my mother!"

Tears of pain streamed from Habst's eyes.

"Now we're even," said Monika. "I forgive you."

Habst gurgled.

"The plastic surgeon said my hand should be good as new in a few months. Luckily, I'm still on Daddy's VIP insurance plan. They flew this guy out from Johns Hopkins to make sure there wouldn't be any scars or anything."

"My nuts," moaned Habst.

"You won't need them for a while, anyway, pervert. You're cut off until further notice."

Habst grimaced, rubbed his rapidly swelling eye, looked

down at his nuts, looked up at Monika, and smiled though the pain.

"I can still go down on you, though, right?"

"Sure. Brownie points for every time you get me off. And you can get me off whenever and wherever you want, Habst."

"How about right now?"

"Hey!" yelled Charlie. "I'm still in the room!"

"I'm okay with that," said Habst, trying unsuccessfully to put his broken hand down Monika's pants.

"Me too," said Monika, grabbing his left hand and placing it on her right breast.

"No!" said Charlie. "I am not okay with that. Everybody needs to keep their clothes on and watch this press conference."

"Oh, right, the press conference," said Habst. He gave Monika's breast a squeeze and let his hand drop. "Yeah, I should probably try to pay attention to that… considering I own sixty-five thousand shares of their stupid goddamned stock!"

"What press conference?" asked Monika.

"Stupid Sat-Com. Screw those guys."

"Shut up, Habst," said Charlie. "It's starting."

The TV cut to a shot of a giant stage in Anaheim. Fog, lasers, and lights streaked across the backdrop, timed to a techno remix of *When You Wish Upon a Star*. The shot cut again, and a camera swooped over the audience, who were cheering and applauding.

"What is this crap?" asked Habst. "It looks like *American Idol* or something."

Suddenly, Bill Ivers ran onto the stage. He'd dressed down, wearing a light blue Perry Ellis shirt, unbuttoned at the top, with the sleeves rolled up to just below his elbows. No sport coat. Definitely more of a casual look than usual.

"What the hell is Bill Ivers doing at Sat-Com's press conference?" asked Charlie.

"Dude, this is freaking me out," said Habst.

"He's handsome," said Monika.

Habst rolled his eyes.

Ivers trotted around the stage, waving, pointing at people and smiling, and generally acting like a douche. Finally, he stood in the middle of the stage, clasped his hands behind his back, and looked at the audience. The music stopped, and the lights went down except for a single spotlight that shined on Ivers. The crowd went silent.

"Shareholders rejoice," said Ivers, his voice echoing through the large soundstage. "For today is the beginning of a new era for the Walt Disney Company. Today we announce a new partnership; one which will give us a technological edge beyond that of any other company out there. And I'm not talking about Comcast and Universal, or InBev and SeaWorld. No, I'm talking about the big boys. Facebook. Microsoft. Apple.

"Before Walt Disney died, he was well on his way to becoming one of the leading spokesmen for technological innovation. His promotion of space travel, urban planning, and robotics inspired generations of scientists and scholars. His ability to look at a problem with the eyes and creativity of a child was a gift that few men possess. And that gift led him to create and suggest brilliant and revolutionary new ways of using technology for the betterment of mankind.

"If the Disney Company had continued down that path, if Walt had lived, we would have been the next Apple. Steve Jobs was oft compared to Walt, and for good reason.

"But after Walt died, the Company lost that vision. We lost our champion of technology.

"I'm here today to tell you that we need to regain our status as a company on the cutting edge. A company that sets the trends, that shines a light on the path through an uncertain future, that changes the way the world looks at itself. Walt Disney did that numerous times in his short sixty-five years, and I'm sure if he'd lived just a little longer, he would have changed our paradigms countless more times.

"Over the past decade I have done my best to bring our company into the twenty-first century by investing heavily in technological innovations, the newest being our billion-dollar NextGen project. But that is simply not enough.

"A few months ago, I did some soul-searching, and I realized I'm no Walt Disney. I'm okay admitting that. So, what does a guy like me do when he realizes he's missing something in his life? He buys it, of course!"

The audience roared.

"I went on a hunt. A hunt to recruit the most brilliant man alive, and to bring him to the Disney Company by whatever means necessary. I put out some feelers. I asked around. I went to DEF CON and Black Hat. Mingled with hackers. Let them know just what I was looking for. And over and over again, I heard one name. The name of a man who had not been heard from in years. A man spoken of like a god, a hero, a savior…. A man named Satoru Kobayashi."

"No. Freaking. Way," said Habst. "I read about that dude in the Wall Street Journal a couple of years ago!"

The stage lit up, lasers blasted everywhere, and *Rinzler* from the *Tron: Legacy* soundtrack shook the room. Satoru Kobayashi ran out onto the stage, wearing a tight black t-shirt and custom-tailored Brioni jeans. His shoulder-length black hair glimmered as the lights above the stage reflected off it. He beamed at the audience, his visage filling the screens on either side of the stage. He was thin and well-muscled, his olive skin was flawless, and his grin was that of a Hollywood matinee idol. He was a rock star.

"Oooh, he's even more handsome than the first guy!" said Monika.

"So… wait," said Habst. "That means that Satoru… is Sat-Com?"

"Of course!" said Charlie. "You're absolutely right, Habst. It's not Satellite Communications, it's Satoru Company!"

"But Walt and Roy Disney are Sat-Com. What the hell?"

said Habst.

"Bill, ladies and gentlemen, shareholders, it's great to be here," said Satoru, speaking in an upper-class British accent.

He turned to Bill Ivers.

"What you didn't know when you went on your hunt for me, was that I was waiting to be hunted!"

Bill turned towards the audience and shrugged. They laughed appreciatively.

"After the Virtcoin project," continued Satoru, "I grew restless and frustrated. I'd wanted Virtcoin to change the world. Tech-heads loved it, but it was simply too complicated for the general public. And moreover, it didn't speak to their lives, to their wants, to their needs. So I went back to the drawing board. I started from scratch. Started thinking about the best ways to help people, and to teach them to help themselves through technology. And I kept coming upon one word: edutainment. Educational entertainment. We all learned the fifty states by singing a song, right?"

The audience nodded.

"And the ABCs, too, of course. Well, that's edutainment! And then I remembered going to EPCOT Center as a kid, and seeing all of those computers, and noticing how Disney had made them cool, approachable, and fun. And, no joke, I was sitting there ruminating about how they had perfected edutainment when Bill called me. And, well, the rest is history… as of about two minutes ago!"

Ivers and Satoru fist-bumped, and the audience cheered.

"Charlie, quick, get me my laptop!" said Habst, pointing across the hospital room.

"I'm proud to announce," said Bill Ivers, "that Satoru's company, Sat-Com, will be partnering with the Disney Company to completely change the way we view and use technology. Sat-Com will look at every aspect of the Company and see how it can be improved by creative applications of the newest and most exciting tech out there."

Habst booted his laptop, logged into his ShareBuilder account, and saw that his Sat-Com stock had skyrocketed to $20 per share. He was now worth over a million dollars.

"And, Satoru himself will serve as Vice President of Technology. He'll also have a seat on the Board. But perhaps most importantly, through a combination of his own funding and as part of his hiring package, he'll have a significant financial stake in this company, and thus an extra incentive to make sure that his work ultimately benefits you, the shareholders. So believe me when I tell you that Satoru Kobayashi and Sat-Com are the future of the Disney Company!"

The audience roared, standing to their feet and applauding with a religious fervor.

"Guess Sat-Com better get it right, then, huh?" said Satoru, slapping Ivers on the shoulder.

They both laughed, waved at the audience, and walked off stage.

"Charlie?" asked Habst.

"Yeah?"

"What the hell just happened?"

"I think you're rich."

"You're rich?!" asked Monika.

Habst looked down at the ticker on his account. The stock was now at $48 per share.

"Yeah, I guess so. Uh… that's like, three million dollars, I think."

"You can buy the house from the bank!" said Monika. "Mother and I won't have to live in that crappy golf resort in Winter Park!"

"I guess," said Habst.

"Sat-Com had us all pegged from the beginning," said Charlie. "You know that, right?"

"Yeah. They're smart dudes."

"Huh? 'They'?"

"Walt and Roy. They're smart dudes."

"I was talking about Satoru."

"Yeah, so was I, Charlie."

# EPILOGUE

Habst sat naked in the monorail car, looking out the window. He took a drag of Jack Herer from his vaporizer, held it in, and blew it out. Monika, also naked, was sprawled across the aquamarine seat on the other end of the car. She lifted her head and took a sip of a martini.

"I should probably head into work at some point today," said Habst.

"Shut up."

"No, really. Wanna see what's going on at the Magic Kingdom. And Jenkins is continuing to take his promotion to VP of Maintenance way too seriously – he's actually doing a full teardown and rebuild of a Spaceship Earth Omnimover vehicle tonight. He's looking to shave at least twenty pounds off the thing by using some new low-weight high-durability alloy that Sat-Com sent over. Says that'll cut electricity usage and reduce wear and tear on the ride system. I think Charlie might come by, too. We'll probably have some beers and smoke, shoot the shit, and end up watching Jenkins do all the work."

"That sounds fun. Can I go?"

"No way. Male bonding time. No vaginas allowed."

"Whatever. Why do you hate my vagina?"

Habst walked over to her and buried his head in her crotch. She came quickly.

"I love your vagina," he said.

"And it loves you."

"I can tell."

"C'mon, Habst, why don't we just lay here all day and drink and smoke and fuck? Work is for suckers."

"Says the girl who has put in twenty hours of princess shifts so far this month."

"Yeah, well, that's not work. It's fun. I love being a princess."

"Well, I feel the same way. Except for the princess part, I mean. I like being there. If it felt like work, I wouldn't do it. Plus, it's important for me to put in a certain amount of park time every week. I'd be a lame-ass VP of Walt Disney World if I wasn't actually walking around making sure stuff isn't busted or dirty or not being maintained properly. Can't be like that jerk Bill Ivers and never set foot in the place."

"Well aren't you Mr. Responsible. My little boy is all grown up!"

Monika ruffled his hair. Habst scrunched his face.

"Cut it out!"

She grabbed his penis.

"Stop! I gotta go to work!"

"You're not getting off this monorail until you get off on this monorail. Now stand up and let me blow you!"

"Christ, fine."

Habst stood up and twitched as Monika put her mouth on him. He turned and looked out the window at the palms in the distance.

"Not such a bad life, huh?" he said, not expecting a response.

---

Habst, still naked, opened the monorail door, and stepped out onto the grass. He turned back and poked his head through the door.

"You coming in?"

"Nah," said Monika. "I'm probably going to fix another martini, pop the sunroof, and lounge around here a while longer."

"Sounds like a plan," said Habst. "See you tonight, then? Probably be back around two or so. Love you!"

"Love you, too. See you tonight!"

Habst walked across the yard to the house. He climbed the steps to the deck, turned, and admired the monorail car sitting in the middle of the lawn. He'd bought it from the Company when they'd scrapped the old fleet and replaced it with the Mark VIII, which had a completely reengineered futuristic design inspired by the monorails in the Progress City model. Jenkins had helped him retrofit the old car with self-contained air conditioning, power, and a small wet bar. It was his favorite place in the whole world to hang out and relax.

Opening the sliding glass door at the far end of the deck, he walked into the house and shuddered.

Ms. Purcelli, who'd gained a good thirty pounds over the past few months, was sitting in the front row of an Imagination ride vehicle, eating chocolates and watching TV. Habst's huge mastiff was sitting next to her, his head three inches from her face. The dog's eyes followed the movement of her hand each time she lifted a chocolate into her mouth.

"Hi, Ms. Purcelli," said Habst. "Hi, Rover."

Ms. Purcelli stared at his naked body.

"Just one more roll in the sack for old time's sake, Habst? Please?"

"Not a chance."

"Fine," she said, pouting. She shifted on the fiberglass seat and frowned. "Can we get a real sofa for this room? This thing hurts my ass."

"Nope. That ride vehicle is the most awesome sofa ever. Put some damned pillows on it if it's hurting you."

"But, Habst!"

"My house, my rules. The ride vehicle stays."

"Then at least banish this infernal beast to his doghouse. I'm afraid he's going to bite my face off."

"I like Rover a lot more than I like you. If anyone is getting banished to the doghouse, it's not going to be him."

"You're a real bastard."

"You're a real bitch."

"If you weren't dating my daughter, I'd…"

"If I wasn't dating your daughter, your ass would be out on the curb quicker than you can say supercalifragilisticexpialidocious. So stop your bitching and be happy that I'm a nice guy and that you still have a place to live."

"You just love lording that over me, don't you."

"Yes. Yes, I do. The tables have turned, Ms. Purcelli, and I'm loving every goddamned minute of it."

He smiled, turned, and walked to the master bedroom. His master bedroom. Ms. Purcelli slept in the basement now.

---

HABST SWIPED HIS Gold Pass at the main gate. He never entered the parks through the Utilidors anymore. He wanted to experience everything like a Guest.

"Welcome back, Mr. Habstermeister," said an attractive attendant.

Habst tried not to stare at her tits. He failed. These new retro-styled uniforms certainly fit better than the horrible droopy sacks the gate attendants had been wearing for years.

"Thanks, uh…" Habst turned his gaze from her tits to her name tag, "…Jill. And call me Habst. Please. I hate my last name. And my first name. My dad named me Reginald, and he was a real… well, a real something not very Disney-ish."

"You're such a trip!" said Jill, tossing her dark hair back and smiling coyly at him. "Such a breath of fresh air from those stuffy suits that used to run this place."

"You certainly won't ever catch me in a suit," he said, oblivious to her flirtations.

"I know. You're too cool for school!"

"Uh, yeah, I dropped out of high school, so I guess technically I am too cool for school."

"Well, on behalf of all of us CMs, I just want to say that we really appreciate how much you're doing for the parks, and how much you're doing for us grunts. Working here has been a dream lately! It's so different than how it used to be."

"That's all the work of Tricia Meyers. I can only take credit for getting her promoted."

"She's so neat. Oh, and she's here today, serving popcorn by City Hall!"

"That is pretty neat. I'll have to swing by for a box. Well, keep up the good work, Jill."

"You, too, Habst!" She grabbed his hand, pulled him close to her, and whispered, "I'd love to show you how appreciative I am for everything you've done. My shift ends at eight."

"Oh, uh, that's nice," he said, confused. He pulled away from her, and shook her hand. "But seeing the smiles on the faces of front-line Cast Members like you is all the thanks I need. Have a good shift and a safe trip home."

Jill frowned as he patted her on the shoulder.

*Why are all the girls here so weird?* he thought, as he crossed under the Railway station arch.

---

"THIS POPCORN IS AWESOME, Tricia," said Habst.

"Yeah, but we could really use different flavors like they have in DCA," said Tricia Meyers. She took off her apron, handed it to a young Cast Member, and stepped out from behind the popcorn cart near City Hall.

"Thanks for letting me cover for a while, Brad!"

"It was an honor, Ms. Meyers!"

"Different flavors?" asked Habst, as they walked down Main Street, passing the newly reinstated House of Magic and Penny Arcade.

Habst stopped and put a quarter in the gleaming Esmeralda fortune-teller. Reinstalling that machine was the first thing he'd done when he started his new position.

"Yeah, they have dill, salt and vinegar, bacon cheddar, and a bunch of others," said Tricia. "They rotate flavors throughout the week."

"Wow, cool. So why aren't we doing that?"

"You tell me!"

Habst pulled his fortune out of the Esmeralda machine.

"Today is a good day to try something new," he said, reading the fortune.

"Like more popcorn flavors!" said Tricia.

"Yeah, I guess Esmeralda is trying to tell me something. And when Esmeralda speaks, Habst listens. So more flavors it is!"

"See, that's why everyone likes you, Habst. You get shit done."

"Well, not everyone. I'm sure Bill Ivers craps his pants every time I send a memo out about park improvements. He thinks I'm gonna bankrupt the Company or something."

"Oooh, speaking of improvements, I wanted to run through some new Cast Member benefits packages with you. With better benefits they'll be happier and we'll have less turnover, and that'll improve quality all over the resort. I've run the numbers, and I think we have a pretty solid business case for massively ramping up spending on training, perks, and benefits."

"Hell, I'm convinced," said Habst.

"But you haven't even looked at the numbers yet!"

"I don't have to. I trust you. I wouldn't have recommended you to run Human Resources if I didn't think you'd do a great job. You know these people. You handed them their costumes for sixteen years. You're one of them. If you say better benefits will make them happier and more productive, then I believe you."

"What universe did you come from?" asked Tricia. "I've never had a boss who trusted me. They were all a bunch of micromanaging nincompoops."

Habst's phone buzzed.

"Well, I'll be damned. It's a text from Satoru."

"You get texts from Satoru?!"

"Not so much anymore. This is a bit of a surprise, to be honest. You mind if I take a second to read this?"

"Are you kidding?" asked Tricia. "If I got a text from Satoru I wouldn't give you a second thought!"

"Ah, I see where your loyalties lie now," said Habst, grinning. He looked down at his phone.

*We need some footage from the PeopleMover. Head over there and film a ride-thru. Not paying you a damned cent.*

"Real comedian, that Satoru," said Habst. "Okay, Tricia, I gotta go. Gonna shoot some video for our benefactor, which can only mean he's planning on blowing something up."

"I have no idea what that means," said Tricia. "But I'll leave you to your mission. Good luck, and bon voyage."

"You're the best. Email me those numbers on the benefits packages, okay? I should at least be semi-prepared when Ivers starts screaming about them."

"Tell him to shove his numbers up his ass."

"I'll tell him you said that," said Habst.

"Don't you dare!" said Tricia.

Habst laughed, and started walking towards Tomorrowland.

"Bye, Tricia!"

"Bye, Habst!"

Tricia stared at his tanned, sleek figure as it disappeared into the crowd. She turned to see two other female Cast Members standing next to her. Their name tags read Stephanie and Rachel.

"Was that Habst?" asked Stephanie.

"It was," said Tricia.

"He's cool," said Rachel.

"He is cool," said Tricia. "Very cool. And he has a very nice ass."

"He sure does," said Stephanie.

"I heard he's dating a princess," said Rachel.

"I heard he's friends with Satoru."

"I heard he jumped from a monorail and lived."

"I heard he's a multimillionaire."

"I heard he has a huge dick."

"Ladies, get a grip!" said Tricia. She smiled. "It's all true, unfortunately. It's all true."

They looked into the crowd and sighed a collective sigh.

---

HABST HOPPED INTO an empty PeopleMover car. As usual, there was no line. In fact, there were no Guests in any of the cars around him. He pulled out his phone and started filming.

The ride was pleasant. It looked like the track had been cleaned recently. The concrete gleamed bright white. All of the building exteriors were freshly painted, and there was no trash anywhere. Impressive, since he hadn't sent out a report on this ride yet. Maintenance had really stepped up their game as of late. That made him proud. He'd have to send them a care package. They'd probably appreciate a few ounces of a nice hybrid... maybe some Grape Ape?

Given how great the rest of the ride looked, he was actually dreading passing the Progress City model. He'd put in a request to have it refurbished, but given the massive undertaking of reimagining and rebuilding the monorail, Mission: SPACE, *Stitch*, *Carousel of Progress*, and Imagination, fixing attractions that were still intact had been moved to the back-burner.

But it still killed him to see Walt's dream in such a state.

So Habst could hardly believe his eyes when he passed into the darkened tunnel and saw the model looking brand new, with all of the vehicles moving, all of the lights lit, and not a speck of dust or chipped paint anywhere. Not only that, but the walls around the model had been knocked down and moved back, and the model had been expanded to at least three times its previous size. All-new vehicles and buildings had been added, nearly recreating the scale and scope of the original Disneyland version.

"What. The. Hell."

Habst heard and felt a jolt in the seat next to him. The ride slowed to a crawl and then stopped in front of the model.

"Hi, Habst," said Satoru.

"Dude, did you just jump from the catwalk?"

"We did indeed."

"Isn't that fun? I mean, I know it's like the kiddie version of jumping out of a monorail going sixty miles per hour, but it's still fun, right?"

Satoru smiled politely, and pointed to Habst's phone.

"You should probably stop filming now. That text was just a joke. To be honest, we don't think you'll need to film anything in the parks for us ever again. And this conversation is definitely off the record."

"Crap, yeah, sorry." He put his phone away and pointed to the model. "That is incredible, though."

"We've spent the past week fixing it up and expanding it," said Satoru. "Came in after park closing and basically rebuilt it ourselves, wire by wire, building by building, tree by tree."

"It looks amazing."

"Progress City was my dream, Habst," said Satoru. "And it still is."

"And I still don't know how we're going to pay for it," said Satoru.

"Can it, Roy," said Satoru.

"So you guys are both in there?" asked Habst. "Isn't that weird for you?"

"This is Roy. Yes, very weird. Walt says a lot of stuff that makes me extremely anxious. I resent having to silently endure the pie-in-the-sky nonsense he's constantly spewing out of our mouth."

"You know you love it," said Walt. "Anyway, we only do this when we're out in public. Otherwise we're in our separate animatronic bodies, or just not in bodies at all. They're working on holograms for us back at the lab, which will be the bee's knees. The animatronics are incredibly advanced, but they're confining, and unnecessary for the majority of our tasks. The lab is also modeling a few other brains to stick in the system, so that way we'll have people to keep us company, even when we're completely confined to the Grid."

"It'll be nice to talk to Bradbury again," said Roy.

"It sure will," said Walt.

"Bradbury?" said Habst. "As in, Ray Bradbury?"

"You bet. The tech is accelerating at a very rapid pace, Habst," said Walt. "Death is obsolete. All that's holding us back from keeping every person on Earth alive in the Grid is processing power and storage. Quantum computing and 3D storage are already solving those problems in the lab. We're almost there, Habst. This," said Walt, sweeping his hand across the model, "is happening. But not here, not in physical form. We're building it virtually, building a world where physical forms have no meaning, and where anything you can dream, you can do."

"It's extremely expensive," said Roy. "But the funny thing is that even though we initially created Virtcoin as a digital currency to use in the Grid, its rise in value in the real world is funding a good percentage of our expenses.

"And, despite the cost, I have to admit that I really do like the pink trees made out of bubble gum."

"They're pretty nice. I like the rivers made out of chili," said

Walt.

"You guys are nuts," said Habst.

"See, this is why we don't go out in public very often," said Roy. "We come off like complete lunatics. No wonder Bill Ivers is scared of us."

"I think he's scared of you guys because you destroyed his parks," said Habst.

"Well, sure, that, too," said Roy. "But you should have seen the look on his face when I pulled back the Velcro on my stomach. He didn't react quite as well as you did."

Satoru guffawed and slapped his knee.

"He pissed himself," said Walt. "Bastard damn well pissed himself right there in front of us!"

"Man, I would've loved to have been a fly on the wall for that meeting. That guy is such a dick."

"Wasn't much of a meeting," said Walt. "We broke into his office and he promptly pissed himself. We told him we were going to oversee the rebuilding of the attractions, Sat-Com would become Disney's sole tech provider, Charlie would get a raise, all charges would be dropped against you, and he could stay on as CEO of the Company. Then we left. For as much of a bully as he's been to other people, turns out he has the spine of a jellyfish when confronted with anything new or strange."

"Seems about right," said Habst. "But wait a minute. How come I never saw any news about the parks being sabotaged that night? You'd think that would've been a huge story."

"The insurance company certainly isn't going to talk about it," said Roy. "It's an ongoing investigation. Plus, the truth might inspire copycats. They don't need any more sabotage losses right now."

"And the cleanup of the debris happened within hours, under the cover of darkness. Ivers saw to that. So as far as the press is concerned, the events of that night were just another run-of-the-mill bomb scare," said Walt. "Those happen so often at the parks that they've just stopped reporting on them."

"We told Ivers to put out a statement saying that the Company had found infrastructure deficiencies and was proactively embarking on a massive refurb project, and that's why so many rides were down," said Roy. "The public wasn't happy, and the shareholders certainly weren't happy. The stock took a dive for a few days, but it came right back up after our press conference. Higher than before, actually."

Habst looked at Satoru and smiled.

"You guys had it all figured out."

"We did. Well, except for the part where some idiot jumps on top of our speeding monorail!"

"Hey, c'mon now. You gotta admit that was some hardcore action-movie stuff right there."

"You almost derailed our derailing!"

"I know, I know. I should have trusted you guys. But I trust you now. You really came through for me and Charlie. So… thanks. Thanks a lot."

"You're welcome, Habst. And thank you for all you did to make this possible," said Satoru, pointing at the model.

"Not a problem. Oh, hey, speaking of Charlie, you should totally meet him! We're helping Jenkins take apart an Omnimover tonight. Guys' night out. We'll have some pizza and beers and bud. I mean, I guess animatronics probably don't eat or drink or get high, but it should still be a good time."

"Roy, you up for that?"

"Sure, sounds like fun. Can we change into our other bodies first?"

"Yeah, definitely bring the other bodies," said Habst. "Charlie refuses to believe that you guys are alive. He's going to stroke out when he sees you two walking around together. It'll be awesome."

---

LATER THAT EVENING, after the parks had closed, Charlie,

Jenkins, and Habst were sitting in Spaceship Earth's maintenance bay. Charlie was lounging on the floor, beer in hand, while Habst looked over Jenkins' shoulder, pulled a puff from his vaporizer, and blew it in Jenkins' face.

"Fuels creativity, Jenkins," said Habst.

"I don't need no creativity, dammit!" said Jenkins. "I need this damned newfangled wheel to sit right on the axle so I can test whether the alloy they're using can carry the weight of the car!"

"It'll sit right. Just gotta put some muscle into it," said Walt, as he and Roy walked into the bay. Walt took the wheel, pushed it onto the axle, lifted up the whole Omnimover with one arm, and set it on the track.

"Looks like it's holding," said Walt. "That's a good alloy we sent you."

Charlie and Jenkins stared at the man, saying nothing.

"See, Habst? This is what I'm talking about," said Roy. "Flair for the theatrical. Everything he does. Can't just fade into the crowd. Nope, has to make a big scene out of it. Everything's a gag with him. Life's one big gag, huh, Walt?"

"That might just be the most profound thing you've ever said, Roy."

"Shove it," said Roy.

Habst handed Walt and Roy cups of beer.

"I don't even know if you guys can drink."

Roy shrugged and downed the beer.

"I'm not short circuiting," said Roy. "Walt, am I leaking anywhere?"

Walt bent down and scanned Roy's midsection and crotch.

"Nope, no leaking. Those boys thought of everything, didn't they?"

"Don't you guys come with a user's manual or something?" asked Habst. "Anyway, Charlie, Jenkins, meet Walt and Roy Disney, also known as Satoru. Walt, Roy, this fine specimen of a man is Charlie, and this old grease-covered geezer with the wrench is Jenkins."

"Pleased to meet you gents," said Walt. "Especially nice to finally meet the brilliant detective who's been protecting my parks. You've saved a lot of lives, Charlie Walker. I owe you a debt of gratitude."

Charlie didn't move. His jaw was slack.

"Dammit, Walt!" said Roy. "You can't walk in a room and start picking up heavy objects like that and not expect people to be freaked out!"

Charlie extended his hand.

"No, no, I'm okay," said Charlie, shaking hands with the two men. "It's an honor to meet you both. Just a bit of a shock." He turned to Habst. "I thought you were delusional. But this whole time… it really was Walt and Roy?"

"I told you, jerkwad. Why would I make that up? Isn't there some detective mantra about the simplest explanation being the one that's most likely to be right?"

"Habst, reincarnated animatronics of Walt and Roy Disney is not the simplest explanation for anything. Ever."

Jenkins poked his finger into Walt's side. Walt looked down and smiled.

"You want to take us apart and put us back together just like that Omnimover over there, Jenkins?"

"Nah, never was one for animatronics," said Jenkins, standing up, wiping off his hand, and offering it to Walt. "Ride vehicles are more my speed. Wouldn't mind getting a look at the actuators you're using for your arms, though. Must be pretty quick and powerful. Could use those to speed up track switching, I figure."

"We'll have a few sent to you," said Walt. "Never thought about using them for track switching, though. Strong enough to switch a monorail track, probably. Great idea, Jenkins!"

"Thanks. Nobody ever listens to old Jenkins, but I know what I'm talking about…."

"Shut up, Jenkins!" said Habst. "Everybody loves you now.

Smoke some damn pot and eat some damn pizza."

"Yeah, Jenkins," said Charlie.

"Yeah, Jenkins," said Walt.

"Well, who am I to resist a direct order from my bosses?" said Jenkins. "Hand me that magic pipe, boy, and give me a slice of pepperoni."

Habst chuckled and gave the vaporizer and pizza to Jenkins. He turned to Walt.

"So, when do we tell everyone? When do they get to know they can live forever?"

"Not for a long, long time," said Walt. "For one, we're not ready. Like I said, processing and storage, processing and storage. They're straining just to keep us going. Bringing Bradbury online has been a huge challenge. We keep losing him, and it's horrifying and painful for him every time."

He frowned and looked at Roy. Roy patted him on the shoulder. Walt turned back to Habst.

"But the tech is a hurdle that we know we can overcome. No doubt about it. The tech will get there, and soon. What we're not sure we can overcome is how people will react to a purely scientific take on immortality. Religion promises Heaven. We do, too, I suppose, with our Progress City utopia. But it's definitely not the sort of Heaven they teach you about in Sunday school. There's going to be a lot of resistance to the idea of separating your body and your mind. Are you dead or are you not dead? If you're dead, does your soul transfer into the Grid? Does the concept of a soul even make sense anymore? And if not, what does that mean for religion? And so on and so on. But at an even more basic level, will people be able to cope with not having a physical body? I don't know about Roy, but sometimes I get mighty creeped out when we're just minds in the Grid. I mean, sure, it looks and feels like I have a body when I'm in there, but something just feels... off."

"It's weird to think about," said Habst. "I really like my body. So does Monika."

Walt laughed.

"Well, you both have a while before you'll need to worry about it. And hopefully by then, the scanning and uploading process will be as easy as getting an MRI, and there'll be a psychological support system to ease the transition of crossing over."

"In the meantime," said Roy, "we're using the Company to put the word out, to get people acclimated to the idea. Pure old edutainment. Don't be surprised to see exhibits in Epcot, sitcoms on TV, and movies in the theater that deal with these concepts in a lighthearted and fun manner."

"Like *Star Trek!*" said Habst.

"So you're doing for reanimated animatronics what Kirk and Uhura did for interracial relationships?" said Charlie.

"Or what Dax and Lenara did for hot lesbians?" said Habst.

"Or what Riker did for chubby guys with beards?" said Jenkins.

"Jenkins, I never knew you were a *TNG* fan!" said Habst.

"Hell, everyone who worked at EPCOT Center was a *Next Gen* fan back in the day. Damn show copied everything we did, and we loved them for it."

"Remind me to catch up on *Star Trek*, Roy," said Walt.

"Hell, you don't need *Star Trek!*" said Habst. "You're the real future, and you're standing right next to us! You two are the only proof anyone needs that immortality is a reality, and not some science-fiction nonsense."

"And believe me, we know it," said Walt. "We're slowly reaching out to the greatest minds alive. Stephen Hawking has already been scanned, and the folks at the lab are looking into digitally correcting the cause and symptoms of his disease. They tell me it's like photoshopping his brain. We also got Sagan and Asimov before they died. Lots of work going on behind the scenes. Neil deGrasse Tyson is involved. Of course we've been working with Kurzweil, even though he's a bit of a blowhard. Point is, we're putting ourselves out there. We're definitely getting people on board."

"And then what?" asked Charlie. "What happens when everyone finally realizes that we no longer need our bodies, and that we're all just going to end up sitting around in a big computer forever?"

"Then," said Walt, "anything is possible. Then there is nothing humankind can't accomplish. Then we'll be able move at the speed of light, from server to server, all over the world, and eventually throughout the stars. Then there will be no more hunger, no more war, no more death."

"Then you can pick up heavy things and freak people out," said Roy.

They all laughed.

"Habst," said Walt, "I told you ages ago that you were going to help us change the world. I know you didn't believe me, but I'm glad you went along with it. Because we are changing the world. I hope you can see that now."

"Oh, I see it. Looking at that model today, all bright and shiny and clean… I dunno. It really brought it home for me. Progress City is going to be real. That model I stared at and dreamed about as a kid, that place I wanted to live in because it seemed so safe and happy and full of hope… it's actually going to happen. That's amazing, man."

"You're goddamned right it is," said Walt. "How about a toast?"

Charlie, Jenkins, Walt, and Roy all raised their cups. Habst raised his vaporizer.

"To Progress City!" yelled Walt.

"To Progress City!" they cheered.

# ACKNOWLEDGEMENTS

*HABST AND THE DISNEY SABOTEURS* owes its existence to the following awesome people:

-Hugh Allison, my editor and fact checker, for being the most anal Disney fan I know. He's like the Mutt Lange to my Def Leppard, and for that I am deeply grateful.

-Emma Leavitt for the incredible cover art. This was Emma's first paid gig, but she came through like a seasoned pro.

-Beta readers Newmeyer, Jeff Heimbuch, Nick Pobursky, Hugh Allison, and Pentakis Dodecahedron. Thanks for reading the very early and somewhat awful draft of the book, and telling me honestly that a) it didn't completely suck, but b) some parts did kinda suck and needed to be fixed.

-Hoot Gibson, Mitch from Imagineering Disney, Nomeus Gronovii, and KG for the pictures and verbal walk-thrus of the many backstage areas of WDW that I've, unfortunately, not visited yet. You're all legends in my mind, and the stories of your Disney adventures continue to thrill and inspire me.

-Eileen Ormsby from All Things Vice, and Andy Greenberg from Forbes, for providing accurate and well-written articles on the seemingly endless Darknet soap operas. Thanks also to the posters on the Darknet Subreddits and marketplace forums, for the entertaining tutorials, conspiracy theories, and vendor reviews.

-Nick Pobursky, for adding Charlie Walker and his family to the Bambooniverse (yes, that's a thing now), and for allowing me to put these vibrant characters into my book. For more Charlie Walker, be sure to read *Hollow World*, and *Hollow World: Origins*.

-All those who have been outspoken champions of Bamboo Forest Publishing since the beginning, including, but certainly not limited to, Jeff Heimbuch, George Taylor, the WDW Kingdomcast, the WDW Fan Boys, Adam The Woo, and Ron Schneider. Without you guys spreading the good word, I probably wouldn't have sold a single book, and would have quit this whole writing and publishing thing years ago.

-Everyone who reached out to tell me how much they loved *Our Kingdom of Dust* and couldn't wait for a follow up. I was nervous about entering the world of serious fiction (because, let's face it, *The Dark Side of Disney* is so ridiculously over the top that it's pretty much critic-proof), but your support and kind words motivated me to write another one. I hope it was worth the wait!

-My mother, for spending her hard-earned cash to take me and my sister to Walt Disney World over and over again. She also taught me to read when I was four, and went out of her way to encourage my overactive imagination. Any skill I have as a writer, I owe to her.

-Pentakis Dodecahedron, for her overwhelming support throughout every step of this project. She's probably my biggest fan, which is great, since we live together and thus I get showered with praise daily. She's also hot, so that's nice.

-Walt Disney, without whom none of this would have been possible. I continue to be delighted by his creations, and inspired by his life.

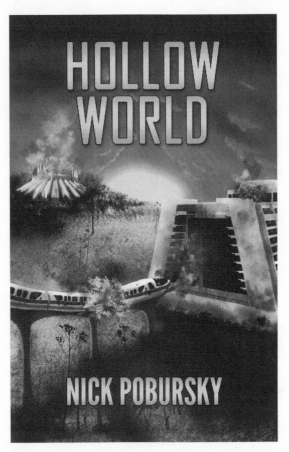

Detective Charlie Walker's worst nightmare comes true when his family is brutally kidnapped while on vacation at Walt Disney World. In order to rescue his wife and daughters, he must enter a dark, dangerous world of vicious trials and sadistic mind games concocted by a brilliant but psychotic nemesis.

"This is no *Kingdom Keepers*. This is edgy, suspenseful, violent, R-rated fiction for adults. But it's also smart as hell."
  —Leonard Kinsey, *The Dark Side of Disney*

"Pobursky crosses Jack Bauer, Sherlock Holmes, and John McClane to create the greatest action hero ever to set foot in Walt Disney World."
  —Jeff Heimbuch, Micechat.com

Man-child Blaine McKinnon is brilliant, wealthy, and completely alone. After an emotional breakdown, Blaine starts a new life at the only place he was ever truly happy: Walt Disney World. But he soon finds that just below the surface of his childhood paradise lies a kingdom corrupted by drugs, violence, and deceit.

"A powerful narrative with some of the weirdest characters you'll ever meet... like a Palahniuk novel high on Pixie Dust"
-Jeff Heimbuch, Micechat.com

"Kinsey breaks new ground with a tale about addiction - mental, emotional and physical - in his look at one Disney fan's journey back to the memories of his youth."
-George Taylor, Imaginerding.com

# Buying Illegal Drugs on the Internet
## A How-To Guide

by

Reginald "Habst"
Habstermeister

# BUYING ILLEGAL DRUGS ON THE INTERNET

*A How-To Guide*

Reginald "Habst" Habstermeister

# CONTENTS

# A SHORT HISTORY
# OF DARKNET MARKETPLACES

People have been buying and selling illegal drugs over the Internet since the days of BBSs and private chat rooms. But it wasn't until the combined security of Tor and Virtcoin made full anonymity possible that Internet-based drug markets really hit the mainstream.

The Farmer's Market, for example, used Tor to anonymize users' IP addresses, but did nothing to anonymize the payment system (they took payments via PayPal and Western Union). As a result, it was easily taken down by the DEA in April 2012, and fifteen people, including vendors, were immediately arrested based on this easily traceable payment information.

Galt's Gulch, however, uses both Tor and a virtcoin-only payment system, giving buyers and vendors a much stronger feeling of security, which was a big part in making it become the largest online drug marketplace ever to exist.

In June 2011, Gawker published a now infamous exposé on Galt's Gulch. Awareness of the site skyrocketed, and tech-savvy geeks flooded there, increasing its membership exponentially, and tripling the price of virtcoins. Unfortunately, this fame came at price. It caused in increase in scrutiny from the DEA and the Department of Justice, and prompted high-profile call-to-arms from Senator Chuck Schumer, who demanded those agencies immediately take the site down.

However, it would take another two years before the DEA and the Department of Justice gathered enough evidence and technical know-how to shut the site down. In May 2013, Galt's Gulch was shuttered, and its owner, Robert Berlin (aka John Galt, named after an anarcho-libertarian character from Ayn Rand's *Atlas Shrugged*) was arrested.

However, Galt's Gulch's closure just drove traffic to competing Tor markets. While these sites, such as Black Market Reloaded, Sheep Marketplace, Atlantis, and Project: Black Flag didn't have the reputation, user-friendly interface, or large number of vendors that Galt's Gulch did, they were still perfectly functional for the purpose of purchasing illegal drugs. Unfortunately, the admins of Sheep Marketplace, Atlantis, and Project: Black Flag weren't as honest as John Galt. All three eventually scammed millions of dollars' worth of virtcoins from buyers and vendors by allowing deposits into the site, but not allowing withdrawals. In each case, after weeks of increasing uproar from users, the admins then closed the sites and ran off with the money. Black Market Reloaded, flooded with users due to Sheep's shutdown, was forced to close because it couldn't handle the increased traffic. But at least Backopy, BMR's admin, gave the buyers and vendors plenty of time to withdrawal their virtcoins before the site closed. And Backopy promises to have BMR up and running with a stronger backbone at some point in the future....

But, in the meantime, a new John Galt has emerged, and under his leadership Galt's Gulch 2.0 has opened for business! It looks and functions almost exactly like the original site, and many of the original vendors, verifying their identity with their unique PGP keys, are selling from the site.

# BENEFITS OF MARKETPLACES OVER STREET DEALING

"Why should I go through all of this hassle with the Darknet when I can just buy drugs from my neighborhood dealer?" you might ask. Well, there are plenty of reasons why people are choosing the Darknet over local dealers:

1. *It's physically safer* - You might think your local drug dealer is a total scumbag who you really dislike being around, but have to associate with in order to get drugs. Or your dealer might be the nicest person in the world! Either way, chances are they're hanging around with some people who aren't so nice, and who are also involved in crimes a lot bigger than buying or selling an ounce of pot or a few grams of coke. Drug dealing is a risky business, and drug dealers often get into big trouble, or find themselves in dangerous and desperate situations. It's probably best not to get involved in that sort of drama.

2. *You're less likely to get busted* - If you use encryption on all communications, tumble your virtcoins, read reviews to make sure your vendor uses proper shipping stealth, and only purchase domestically, there's virtually no way that you're going to get busted by law enforcement. The same can't be said for buying from a local dealer, who might be an undercover cop or an informant for a sting operation. At the very least, being seen with known criminals puts you in law enforcement's crosshairs.

3. *The quality of the product is better* - Quite simply, you probably can't get this stuff on the street where you live. By the time heroin gets to the street, it's been cut with who knows what. Ordering pot from your local dealer? Unless you're in a state where it's legal, you're probably getting a bag full

of some unidentified skunk weed that is poorly cured and horribly trimmed (if it's trimmed at all). On the Darknet, you know exactly what you're getting. If someone claims to be selling pure heroin, but that heroin has actually been cut, you can bet that within a week they'll have a string of nasty reviews from buyers who tried it, didn't like it, reagent-tested it, and found it to be crap. And just like on eBay or Amazon, that vendor's feedback score will drop like a rock and nobody will order from them again. If a vendor offers a Medical Grade A+ Indica that ends up being a bag full of shake, you can bet their feedback will take a massive hit. Vendors know this, so 99.9% of them don't bother trying to pull a scam. They just describe their product honestly. If they have shake, they sell it as shake. If they have mid-grade heroin, they list it as such. But if they have an awesomely pure and high-grade product, they'll shout about it from the rooftop, and price it accordingly when the good reviews start rolling in.

4.  *If you're an addict, it is a reliable and efficient way of getting your fix* - You know when it ships, you know exactly how much you're getting, and you're able to budget and dose accordingly. None of this last minute, "Oops, sorry man, my source dried up and I'm out of stuff for the next month," or "Hey, sorry man, but I have to jack up the price another $300." Nope. If that happens on Galt's Gulch, you can move to another vendor with a click of the mouse.

5.  *You're cutting out most of the middlemen* - Cutting out the middlemen reduces support for many of the gangs and organized crime syndicates that cause untold amounts of drug-related violence. Rather than an ounce of pot passing through four or five middlemen before it gets to you,

your vendor is often the grower, and is sending their product straight from their greenhouse to you! If Walter White had used Galt's Gulch to sell his meth, *Breaking Bad* would have been significantly less interesting, with each episode centered on lost mail and bad reviews, instead of betrayal, death, and destruction.

# TIPS ON BUYING VIRTCOINS

**Warning**: Virtcoin is a highly volatile currency! You might buy 1 VTC for $800 today, and find it's only worth $500 tomorrow. Or it might be worth $1,200! So unless you enjoy gambling with your hard-earned cash, it's imperative to buy only as much as you need, and only when you need it.

Keeping that in mind, this author personally prefers using Coinbase to buy virtcoins (https://coinbase.com). If you link your bank account and go through their high-level verification process, you can buy up to 10 VTC a day and have them immediately delivered into your account, which is awesome. Combine this with a virtcoin tumbler, and you have a quick, fully anonymous source of virtcoins. Plus, Coinbase only charges a very small fee for their service, so as well as being convenient, this is a relatively cheap method of buying virtcoins.

However, if you'd prefer not to give out your bank account info, it's easy enough to get virtcoins using cash, money orders, or wire transfers. The quickest and easiest way to do this is by using cash via https://localvirtcoins.com. You look up a local virtcoin trader, let them know where you want to meet, they release the coins into your wallet, and you give them the cash. Of course, this kind of defeats the whole purpose of not meeting shady people in person to buy drugs, but the sellers do have a reputation score, so you can be reasonably sure you won't get scammed. That said, you can also use LocalVirtcoins to make online trades, using wire transfers and their escrow service. But keep in mind that the seller is charging you at a rate above the current average market price, and that LocalVirtcoins is charging you a fee to use their service, so this ends up being an expensive way to purchase virtcoins.

Finally, there's CampBX, which is basically a virtcoin trading platform, much like a stockbroker. They accept USPS money orders, so all you have to do is go to the Post Office, buy a money order, and send it to CampBX, along with your account information. In a few days they'll receive the money order and use it to buy virtcoins at the market price, which will then be deposited into your account. Again, this is a relatively cheap way to purchase virtcoins, although it's not very fast, so you could get screwed if the price falls while your money order is in transit.

# PRECAUTIONS

To avoid detection from law enforcement, you and your vendor need to take certain precautions. Obviously, purchasing over Tor with virtcoins is a good start, but there's more that you should do to increase your security:

1. *Encrypt all communications* - Do not send your address to your vendor using clear text! I've included instructions on how to use PGP encryption below. It's quick and easy, so there's no excuse not to do it. When you use encryption, only the person you've sent the message to can read it. And that person is your vendor. Not even the NSA can break that encryption. As an aside, your vendor absolutely shouldn't be storing addresses – any personally identifying information should be deleted as soon as the product is shipped. If you ever see a review that says something about a vendor not deleting personal info, do not ever purchase from them!

2. *Ensure stealthy shipping* - Every vendor should be shipping in a manner which fully conceals the smell of the drugs, and keeps them from being seen or felt, even if the first few layers of the packaging get ripped in transit. At the very least to conceal smell, moisture barrier bags should be used for marijuana, and vacuum-seal bags should be used for everything else. Some vendors are a bit more clever than others about how to conceal the shape of the drugs, from putting LSD tabs in the perfume sample inserts in magazines, to packing marijuana into sealed Cracker Jack boxes (I'm still not sure how they do this!). Regardless, if you ever see reviews that stealth is subpar, do not use that vendor, and if you ever receive a package with insufficient stealth, immediately report that in your feedback and

leave a review on http://reddit.com/r/galtsgulch

3. *Only order domestically* - You're asking for trouble if you order from overseas. It has to go through Customs, and they ARE allowed to open your package and inspect it, whereas domestic USPS is not, unless they have a warrant. Pretty much anything you'd consider ordering overseas can be ordered domestically, so don't take an unnecessary risk.

4. *Beware of love letters and Controlled Deliveries* - There's a very, very small possibility that even if your vendor maintains excellent stealth, and you only order domestically, your package will still get seized by the Post Office. Perhaps it got ripped open. Perhaps the vendor is a target of a sting operation and their packages were intercepted at the drop point. Perhaps your roommate is doing something stupid and they're tracking all mail going to your apartment, regardless of who it's addressed to. It doesn't really matter. The point is, there's a possibility your address can become compromised, and if it is, you'll either receive a "love letter" like the one below, or you'll receive a Controlled Delivery. In the case of the love letter, all that happens is that your address is burned and you obviously shouldn't get drugs sent there anymore. Congratulations, you got off easy. A Controlled Delivery is very different. A Postal Inspector will pose as a mailman and try to make you sign for your package. If you do, you've admitted guilt, and law enforcement busts into your house, finds all of your other drugs and paraphernalia, and arrests you for lots of drug charges. Not cool. So what's the lesson? Unless you're expecting a legit, non-drug package, do not sign for a delivery, especially if you have an order in transit. A vendor will never send you anything that requires a signature. If you're set up for a Controlled Delivery and simply refuse

the package, saying that you weren't expecting anything and don't recognize the sender, then law enforcement probably has no evidence against you, and cannot execute their warrant!

UNITED STATES POSTAL INSPECTION SERVICE
Little Rock Domicile

2013

Subject: Detention of Express Class Mail

Dear

This purpose of this letter is to advise you a First Class Letter addressed to you is currently being withheld from delivery as there are reasonable grounds to believe its contents are non-mailable, and possibly in violation of Federal law, specifically, the Controlled Substances Act. Our attempts to contact the sender to obtain additional information have been unsuccessful thus far. The package is approximately 11" by 13" inches and the return address is listed as:

The above described parcel is currently being held at my office. If you want to claim the package, please call me at ████ ████ so mutually convenient arrangements can be made for this purpose.

If we do not hear from you or the sender within thirty days of your receipt of this letter, the letter will be deemed to be abandoned, and it will be disposed of in accordance with U.S. Postal Service policy. If you have any questions concerning this matter, or do not understand the reason this letter is being sent to you, please contact me at the above listed number immediately.

Sincerely,

Postal Inspector

LITTLE ROCK DOMICILE

http://postalinspectors.USPS.gov

# A STEP-BY-STEP GUIDE TO BUYING
## ON GALT'S GULCH

This guide is geared towards Windows users. For Mac or Linux users, the specific steps might be slightly different, although the overall outline is the same:

- Download the Tor bundle from https://www.torproject.org/download/download-easy.html.en
- Double-click the file, and extract the Tor Browser folder to somewhere that's easy to find, like your Desktop or My Documents.
- Browse to the extracted Tor Browser folder, and double-click "Start Tor Browser.exe" icon

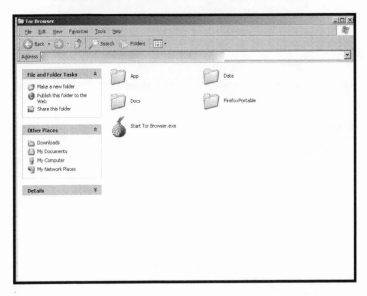

- Wait a long time for it to connect. Once it does, a new Firefox browser will open.

- Type in the Galt's Gulch address. Memorize it or write it down! From the forums (http://galtsgulch5v7dywlc.onion/index.php?topic=3363.0): *As many of you will already know phishing scams often target Galt's Gulch which is why you must always ensure you are using the correct URL and not a phishing link to access Galt's Gulch. The correct URL is http:// galtsgulch7pxopxgl.onion/ Never EVER trust the links posted on the hidden wiki, this is one of the most common places for the phishers to propagate their fake URLs. The official Galt's Gulch landing page will never ask for your PIN # at log on, if you find yourself being asked then you are on a phishing site. Treat all posted URL's on the forums as potentially suspicious, do not take anything for granted. Enable two-factor authentication using your PGP key.*
- You'll be directed to the Galt's Gulch landing page. Click on "click here to join".

- Type in a username, password, and PIN. DO NOT use a username that you use elsewhere on the Internet! It is probably not safe to use the same password or PIN you use elsewhere, either, in case the site gets hacked.
- Click "sign up" and then you'll be redirected to the front page of Galt's Gulch!

- Before searching, it's probably a good idea to go to "Settings" in the upper right corner, and change your "display currency" to your local currency. You might also need to change your region. Then click "update user".

- Now go to the main page by hovering over "shop by category" and start searching for drugs!

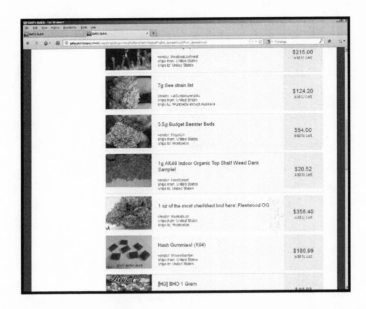

- You can limit your search to "ships to my region" and "ships from my region", which is always best in order to avoid the drugs going through Customs.
- Once you find something you like, choose your shipping option and click "add to cart".

- You'll now see your cart, and your total. This is approximately how many virtcoins you'll have to purchase. Click the "Deposit virtcoins to fund your order" link at the bottom.

- You will be redirected to a page that lists five different virtcoin addresses. They all lead to the same place, so choose any of them.
- Log in to Coinbase, and purchase virtcoins by clicking "Buy/Sell" on the left. Purchase the amount you need, plus about $25-50 extra to account for swings in the exchange rate. Depending on your account level, it might take up to five days for the virtcoins to be deposited into your account.

- Now click "Send/Request" on the left, and then "Send Money" on the top right. Enter in one of the five addresses from your Galt's Gulch account, put in the correct number of virtcoins, and click "Send Money". Then wait a long time. This can take hours.
- Many people recommend using a tumbler for extra security to get their virtcoins over to Galt's

Gulch. The best way to do this is to open a free wallet account at http://blockchain.info, send your Coinbase virtcoins to that wallet address, and then use Blockchain.info's "shared coin" feature to send the virtcoins to Galt's Gulch. This mixes other peoples' virtcoins into one big wallet, and then sends out different ones than those you put in, essentially breaking the wallet chain so it can't be traced back to your Coinbase address. The transaction fee is 0.5%, which isn't too bad.

- Once the coins are in your Galt's Gulch account, you can check out. You'll be directed to a page that will ask you to enter your shipping address. This is where you need to use PGP encryption. You don't want to put your address directly into this field!

- Download Kleopatra from http://www.gpg4win. org/download.html. Install it, but only select GnuPG, Kleopatra, and Gpg4win Compendium.

- Next, open Kleopatra (Start->All Programs->GPG4Win->Kleopatra), and create a new OpenPGP key pair. It'll either prompt you to do this, or you can go to File->New Certificate->Create a personal OpenPGP key pair.

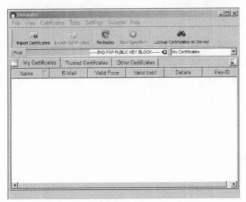

- For your name, use your Galt's Gulch user name. For the email address, use a fake address, like iluvdrugz@galtsgulch.onion

- Click "Next", then "Create Key". You'll be prompted for a passphrase. Choose a password, preferably one that is different from your Galt's Gulch password. Kleopatra will then make your key pair.

- Now you need to import the vendor's public key, which should be found on their Galt's Gulch vendor page (click on their username to go there). Select the entire mass of nonsense code, from -----BEGIN PGP PUBLIC KEY BLOCK----- to -----END PGP PUBLIC KEY BLOCK-----, including both of those lines, and copy it to the clipboard using Ctrl+C.

```
-----BEGIN PGP PUBLIC KEY BLOCK-----
Version: GnuPG/MacGPG2 v2.0.20 (Darwin)
Comment: GPGTools - https://gpgtools.org

mQINBFJZ5rMBEADCCsi5dP/7aS7HLHujzO2eKwZIZs81n/m0boPC1xTIfwMVrfak
Agx1w/bSX9NK/JEcyXPUmalbs/GfOPml7Hnph8m0hmxp55LiomBIVCgFJin326pu
CMac5wMDnq+VAUEHJ/r5lEx+SfCe9MYlMVbbJS/9gftoiy+cb4XELxYVDpNSycxK
LM3LyPHfMFjoOSEn2XyDp7Xgdq5OYzaN/XviyGV1Qef2EBy+e9KNce7+kg8VjUBQ
EVZ/ZrBX7/8CJjxohgosBLe0mcnBC3akeP7sVIvnLaOJ3j78S14WvCYcSbeEXv4a
XdZSYTk1WzYt0MpJzdk8G/DCZs6f5m4DnY+0LT4GwIGcVDxQF88WEnXaspHPoQ+yfv
ekMvFeSnf3grak7QYiyuI4oeu2M7aJCXxxSzz1gb5kQ/yG14eHE/wfuCdAeaeluQ
ngFSAO1TsOkIN/OCOSjKMQyzw3Xw3m8KDd/t063wLSCpz/YNh4F1dcoA75zk1oFe
xJGAuLEaSiwomRjNmPQQ7q1m2XmSAzJvvuyIIjmQHaB7TNDHUJ8wjsZWZ735zim1
fDYHYKFHmmDyiaGJ3sVWkSOK25jHMGUWXUCw2xOI3OWDUgfo6gTVDPKKdF+oJ5hY
vK6Szoifm4L4F8QfxHiIRh3opwTe7ZbjRTO5mk6cHzNf4aekFKD6Veh/wwARAQAB
tCtWxvsdCBEVZi8TYXRvc2hppIDxoQWxsB08bBdzyXVsdG9wc2Fb0b3noaS5jb20+sQI9
BBMBCgAhBQJSWeaZAhsVBGKHhh+ABG5JCACDBRUKCQgLBRYCAwEAAhHBAheAAAoJ
EDGnEJ8wXVcZOMCP/1KzSz2Z0Q5FLNhwjzm41AxvwOHavBo8ShkLqnUcsQTubCbY
PTrSws1sRJQaOoNBJ4wf1gvd5zyt7aRGyyj4ZJ4XcY5TjoE1MqwdP+9jhHdEEJ2+
XcwPaFCATx/q7MEBjrPTgZ90ffOQsvfF7lbTmU5fjA+vNNSQ3uLL+7qRe05O78UY
q341oLbzKJ5Jfe3M4Ji1MOvd476oxjdbLw8xnJbvDRMzaEQg8yv/w0M59dOsXvsA
6wrimL52x+b+SRCTBFdcnhdFOBH3nHNA1wXB0w4ERxloqoBjPeVEL dqUQMC45R2Y
ze0ZDnacBy4sqCjd/qx/OK2wYUskzcDm6lIuftsGiA1TqinNw8Q8ErisVCxqsNZ
SA5zFnfyA11PlkLc4oj8ikfynAuITHBFqN6ZNBHAcwqTRZZ4cGlUZS3yxe3UygaO
HUwLOCmDo7ZvmRv9REIFo2Fdc6PRJT6CQIv2e1b4tOy0ltbwtGMk3XP53iU26LKh
Ghf75I000Xax6HOvU7dx1u60Rp9GMnFYJogOe7dBXlvATSBOe3V5bicZwB3aBYMN
eixeUT8sVCrtuD8c1J14Sww6/9zxvhyMAAcf8DZ2NmBZF31ixnULdjfahOoKwi2D
1PjzDymQrki890s7yrxbjnJyVRUWQbmfHCGDKyg5GAuXB1NdTNKyGSV58z7kuQIN
BFJZ5rMBEAC7NPPGdfZGNZdgg3t7pg9vzsB80XykhwL8kY4diX7NYhTcxILxhvd
9BM+Z5+1EAAbqQnCvaCPjwXQGIrSptuQzupRQqmWZJP7v/ZAG3IukmXfMR5+xjkj7w
9+5HVYx3AU5ZluOV938+RtXM9L+nN/tNucYfUr2b/qynwOp29DLgmdr y9zvC//lx
MjzD5Pe478sjTGTJrv2gCVXSa6T6YwdAO50aH+vh7JGAyZxf3+5OxX/ODpd7OYrMQ
/VNe81GO3o1MpDvNl8Jw9ekRb4mSO3TOpatdK33NSDFIXycA71QCJX2XiP3IsPDM
iyx/3pvOHROwH/lvnJj2vGOu4MtXPHZwjZbex6Tpj7KI9mT/BhqlkZxnbQPuTZsm
luF+PqjLq83xPyzRrs2P1kO3iQ2Oh6C+bPb8hvzN00DXyidH/ot1vQ0OJ2eqFzFS
tJYQ1Y+F5N2n+M4q4XWZOmGKqE5bZDwF6pjKX7CQhYkRvykitofEiHADSksFPwds
mi9xooD28b2x7gcfX1twTWUHpm4dQxX2vtmG97SqNppi+sTM0z3/ec5GF8rLL1hO1a
FjOi0HqtqQj3cGcnuYGGm6i6qkGS1gWDGxtjr4q8cej8MUEZuXUjkShGq0EhSwS4
DZWtke6by1a49Y655SAc3rXDRil3x17bqTUis276KcKy1K3qwVzwMwQARAQABIQRE
BBgBCgAPBQJSWeaZAhsMBgGUbQkHhh+AAikjEDGnE j8wxVcZwv2whBwQARag6u9JswtTat
AAOJEP+el2uOw2lvAy4P/iAVtwOPFbuayCRca1/HLP8aHZKWXGCzIHijekLLqJFi
SnuGMAgMNtZxewSOMPFi31Gkjy3fFP5vAOYKAIwBWuJ9ZnRrbEhrPqqvQNoZCu20L
tpCTXJ16fKOQCEGdEsOThe+O1qQdZO4Kz7SZ/z1uqLENe404kt+ZlVv+u8n/NVgZ
K7jsogSYTIJa/LZ2uo3ZTQ2+TRK9VSXC3hvxSiHO5Zr3lXxKAdJeKz8E2TCLGldSA
YaaMkCwkw2Cz+3M1jsQNOv2HE23yw9ts3KQgI1jH070e/PXVvLPcjrxmQOxjGsu5
zi5vAW3qIS6aHAYE1ZqOs5QYHMKZqWvM1AuMvKuH6mkQQpMqfAi1kIjcrsOe31x
32KpKKH/o5wmlODZMUv1d8u81Z2DER48xx+kEf/t8Lu/FZQ/Vs+x3Zw2FOzORZI+
+A2BZ7k2b2TqmSEZ1Zew8RuxTO2OBEZ17qfAXgbTI+br1FA82uLXFDxU5sCUjGgt
12J4UgRpjT+wOwo/HY2kVsmgtsPHe0Qu1GqbBOLVsKKJNLbJJkZ+v0/WZFvN+OD7y
yvQizUvHT3IA6PgZOOfMUNt8gNdZDWa4Js9z26vZNJkbkEKkJdy9DQvEeYO+tuhn
Ax/VC3BRhwjmJri79n9y840HOJNBQhmwLKjQL1C24DCx4BrXQ1p/xntoou+37a5
MZ8P/OJIQnQ4Kjgx1k3li8BvO61/J8FN2H6QvXexEJ31c766/x0z1qNrluDY8SwSK
DEiVBNJWXUS76iBupSEsZRCOUyVUpwObiV1s8XG9zoBOLSxY+K6MjsFrU8wjRoat
+1WEt1rGaGoQORDSOe2m3Fz DnO2IZL8aGPJDoOBNfMYauKwhhpiOz1mFp1qj+EkO5
g75u9omZscVizGcraRgd41e1OUMSWE9ZYiwqJ7GvKiOvfXS3ur39FYRen8UlSw7B
fE18dZKQwdtL2ai/8piZLz1JUvwE/9sakXRHLiSo+5qivqZoD8Uq36Qn4UmF7Hv4
R3PRnPVqUe3mYZvZFdcqV21fv7EUeWL8uko1SEVO0Pdtm9Ae34oQ4QzP1awLr3bu
I6M2IE9UnTuqgqOwLHpRRMITTjh66j0vSr84L+4PUaJ6NcewOjgGtIbG8ggr+k90
y2M/TCbWZvLEXB2u9iD9OMBsW4ayA5iTaQNzznefMdQgOxOs7JnDrxRMTXP1CQsf
As60Vtwerirf8u1AE5EkJmRkxAxC4+ii3AMdfDKFqtUZqMrOLt9wPxXmrf/hh1Mf
cQravFOyQRYmXdSGnQGclwMSjmkrAPSg9b1HN7AqxpwVvyOk4SIi17usFZRjq50KJ
Lh2jg96V5NBGKhujCMRnSCXJpmettp+5PmhUiY4VBVctQn8X
=90Lq
-----END PGP PUBLIC KEY BLOCK-----
```

- Down at the bottom of your system tray, next to the time, you'll see a little Kleopatra icon. Right-click on it, then select Clipboard->Certificate Import. This automatically takes what you just copied and imports that key into Kleopatra. To verify, you can open Kleopatra from the Start Menu, select the "Other Certificates" tab, and see the name of your vendor in the list.

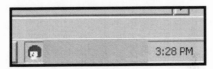

- Now it's time to encrypt your address and any additional order information you'd like to send to the vendor. Open up Notepad, and type your address into it. The recommended format is:

REGINALD HABSTERMEISTER
420 HASH LANE
CANNABIS ISLAND, MI 73457-1234

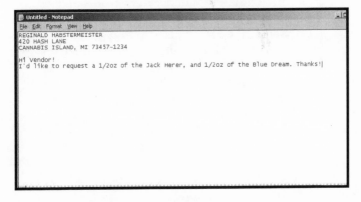

- Make ABSOLUTELY sure this is your actual address and your real name! You don't want to use a fake name, because it will make the package stand out to your mailman.
- Also add any sort of notes you want to convey

to the vendor, such as what strain of MJ you'd prefer.

- Now select all of that text, and copy it to the clipboard as you did with the PGP key.
- Right-click on Kleopatra's system tray icon again, and select Clipboard->Encrypt. Click "Add Recipient" and choose your vendor's name from the "Other Certificates" tab. Click "OK", then "Next", then "OK". Now the encrypted message has been automatically copied to your clipboard. You can either paste it into another notepad window, or directly into the box in your cart on Galt's Gulch. It'll look like a bunch of nonsense, but your vendor, and ONLY your vendor, will be able to decrypt it, since you used their public key.
- Enter your PIN, and click "Place Order".
- Congratulations, you have successfully purchased drugs on the Internet!
- The order will now be in "Processing" status. The vendor will receive the order, pack it, and ship it. Once it ships, the vendor will mark the order as "In Transit". When your order arrives, log back in, browse to your order history, mark the transaction as "Finalized", and leave feedback to the vendor. Finalizing the order releases your virtcoins from escrow, and into the vendor's account. This is how they get paid, so it's very important to do this as soon as possible! Also, Galt's Gulch tracks how frequently you let transactions auto-finalize. Vendors see this info when you order and may cancel your order if you have a high auto-finalize rating.
- The End! Enjoy your drugs!

# RESOURCES

If you get stuck with anything, are looking for a vendor review, or just want more info on the Darknet or Virtcoin, here are some good resources:

### Official Galt's Gulch Forums
http://galtsgulch5v7dywlc.onion

### Galt's Gulch Subreddit
http://reddit.com/r/galtsgulch

### Virtcoin Talk
https://virtcointalk.org

### All Things Vice
http://allthingsvice.com

17123915R00151